She clenched her teeth to keep them from chattering. She was on the edge of blind panic. But she knew that to panic would be a mistake. Possibly a fatal mistake. She had to stay calm, for if Spencer actually had the kind of control over the people at Enlightenment that he wanted her to believe he had, he was presenting her with the opportunity to find out how it was done. This was the information Alice had asked her to get.

Spencer led her back to the dining hall without speaking. The room seemed darker than it had before and strangely quiet. He motioned her toward a side door. "This is my private dining room. Please go in."

She stood uncertainly for a moment. Then pushed the door open. When she turned, Spencer stood in the doorway. The pistol was in his right hand.

"What are you going to do to me?" Stephanie gasped.

"Why nothing, my dear."

"What do you want from me?"

"Nothing. I told you. I'm going to tell you some secrets about Enlightenment. Then you'll forget we ever had this little talk. You'll see. This is for everyone's good."

by the author of

THE CHESAPEAKE PROJECT (1990)

Lodestar
BY PHYLLIS HORN

The Naiad Press, Inc.
1991

Printed in the United States of America on acid-free paper
First Edition

Edited by Ann Klauda
Cover design by Pat Tong and Bonnie Liss
    (Phoenix Graphics)
Typeset by Sandi Stancil

Library of Congress Cataloging-in-Publication Data

Horn, Phyllis, 1938—
    Lodestar / by Phyllis Horn.
        p.   cm.
        ISBN 0-941483-83-5 : $8.95
        I. Title.
PS3558.0686L64   1991
813'.54--dc20
                                                                    90-21906
                                                                    CIP

This is for my own guiding star,
Lady Di

And for my good friends
Ashlea, Brenda, and Pat.
Thanks for cheering loudly!

ABOUT THE AUTHOR

Phyllis Horn lives with her life partner in coastal
Virginia where she is currently employed as a
university professor. She has published a number of
scholarly articles, but writes fiction for fun and
relaxation. She also enjoys boating and bird
watching.

CHAPTER ONE

The courtroom walls reverberated with the angry sound of the man's voice.

"She's a goddamned lesbian!" Greg Rooney screamed. His cold eyes drilled a hole in his ex-wife's face. "What the hell else do you need to know, Judge? I told you she's queer for that whore she's living with. She's my wife and I ought to know her bedroom habits!"

Dr. Stephanie Scott watched Greg Rooney's antics from her seat behind the defense table. What an obnoxious little shit he is! she thought.

When the man stood up he was five-foot-six, but he appeared to be much taller as he reared back arrogantly in the witness chair of the Richmond, Virginia, Domestic Court. A blue-and-white striped seersucker jacket hung loosely on his small frame. Underneath it, the yellow sport shirt looked dingy, like his blond, shoulder-length hair.

Stephanie Scott tried to imagine what it would be like to be married to such a person. Everything about him suggested he was the human equivalent of a rattlesnake, a man coiled up inside himself, waiting to strike. A man who believed that just being male made him more important than God. Stephanie shuddered as he shifted his eyes toward her and narrowed them into slits. It was as if he had heard her thoughts about him. She forced herself not to frown.

The judge seemed momentarily frozen by the audacity of Rooney's outburst. Then she pounded loudly on the desk with her gavel. "Young man, you will hold your tongue in my courtroom and answer only the questions that are put to you!" Her voice was stern but not loud. She had an almost imperceptible foreign accent.

For some moments there was total silence.

Judge Alice Cutter was a veteran of the Domestic Court. She had a reputation for toughness and a no-nonsense approach to the law. The local newspapers called her the South's Iron Maiden and praised her for having no patience with anything that smacked of child or spouse abuse during her years on the bench. Her face was darkly exotic, even handsome. The gray in her hair ran toward silver and her eyes were a piercing, deep blue.

"I want you to listen carefully to me, Mr. Rooney," Judge Cutter continued. "I want there to be no possibility of misunderstanding on your part concerning what I am about to say. I am reversing the joint custody ruling that was made at the time of your divorce and I am withdrawing your visitation rights."

"I'm sorry? What? I think I must not have heard you right," Rooney said, and cupped his ear with his hand. He turned his body in her direction and grinned as if to let her know that nothing she could say would change anything he might do — even if he heard her plainly. Then, to make sure she understood his message, he defiantly stuck out his thin chest and squared his narrow shoulders.

Judge Cutter answered his insolence by speaking even more softly. "You, sir, have been accused of the physical abuse of your former wife and your children. Ample evidence has been presented to this court in the form of photographs and hospital records to convince me of the truth of that accusation. And you can wipe that stupid-looking grin off your face!"

"Judge Cutter . . ." Rooney's lawyer, Andrew Brown, began.

"You'd do well to keep your peace at this point, Mr. Brown, before you make matters even worse for your client," said the judge, without taking her eyes off Rooney.

Brown shook his head conspicuously, but said nothing more. He knew from past experience that there was no point in arguing.

"Mr. Rooney," the judge continued. "The fact that you have come here claiming that your wife is a lesbian in no way changes the fact that you were never a fit husband, or a good father to your children. Many women in your ex-wife's situation are forced to share living quarters with someone else in order to make ends meet. And I am totally unimpressed with your opinion of what her relationship with her housemate may be."

She made a brief note on the pad in front of her, then pointed her pen at Rooney. "Your lawyer has presented a convincing case for your being a victim of parental abuse yourself. I have no doubt that this is true. Abusers have nearly always been abused."

Rooney sneered and quietly muttered, "You bet your butt."

Judge Cutter ignored the remark. "But Mr. Brown's claim that those facts make you blameless, Mr. Rooney, does not sit well with me. In fact, some of the evidence he has presented to this court persuades me that you are a seriously disturbed young man. Dr. Scott's testimony concerning your psychological status puts the cap on the stack, so to speak. Her report states that you are a chronic alcoholic with a history of repeated violence. It suggests that you are a classic psychopath with no morals or ethics. In my opinion, you, sir, and men like you, are a danger to the very roots of civilized society. No defense on earth can excuse what you are."

This time as she spoke, she raked her sharp eyes over the attorney, Andrew Brown, who tried to get lost inside the collar of his Italian silk suit. He grimaced and bit his lower lip.

"In fact," she went on, "I am tempted to *order*

4

you to seek treatment, but since this is the first time, to my knowledge, you have appeared in Domestic Court, I have decided not to. However, I strongly suggest that you do so on your own. If you don't learn to control your temper and your impulsive nature, you will no doubt end up in this court again or in someone else's. It's fortunate for you that Mrs. Rooney is not seeking to prosecute you for your misbehavior."

Rooney's sneer became more pronounced as he heard that piece of news. Andrew Brown had warned him that his ex-wife could file assault charges as part of the custody suit. He tilted his head upward and looked down the sides of his nose at the judge through his bloodshot eyes. "Guess she ain't completely crazy after all," he said under his breath.

"I do not agree with her decision to allow you to keep your freedom," Judge Cutter continued. "But she says she hopes you will be willing and able to pay her some of the alimony and child support that is owed her if you are not in jail. I personally doubt that you will, but that, sir, is her choice. What she has asked is that I issue a restraining order, which I am happy to do."

"Judge, you got this all wrong," Rooney objected, half standing. "They're my kids. And you ain't gonna take 'em from me."

For a brief moment Stephanie thought the judge might throw the pen she held in her hand, but instead she went on in a level tone, ignoring the man again. "Mr. Rooney, I order you to have no further contact with your wife or your children. In fact if you do so, she may have you immediately arrested and put in jail, and, sir, if I hear the case, I shall recommend that they throw away the proverbial key. Do I make myself clear?"

A slow, cocky grin stretched across Rooney's face. "Judge, ma'am, if you please," he said with mock politeness. "You listen up. I made a little mistake, you know. I was drunk. I admit it, but you can't —"

Judge Cutter's eyes flashed as she leaned forward on both elbows. She raised her voice for the first time. "I *can*, Mr. Rooney and I *am!* You are to have *no further contact* with these people for any reason whatsoever! Consider yourself lucky to get off so lightly. Now get out of my court and don't come back!"

Rooney stiffened and uttered a barely audible "Fuck you."

"Mr. Rooney, I can cite you for contempt of court today if time in jail is what you want. Otherwise I have nothing more to say to you."

Rooney's mouth opened briefly, then he shook his head and looked down at his lap where his hands were clenched into white fists.

Judge Cutter pounded again with the gavel, then made a show of gathering up her papers. "This court will reconvene at two o'clock," she said, then looked in Stephanie's direction and smiled. "Dr. Scott, if you have a few minutes, could I see you in chambers?"

* * * * *

The judge's chambers were dark. The room had masculine, heavy furniture and thick drapes that framed the single window and made the room seem stuffy and depressing. On the massive oak desk, a single red rose in a silver bud vase added a small touch of femininity.

Alice Cutter removed her robe and placed it securely on the coat rack. She was wearing a simple white blouse and black skirt underneath. She was tall and stylishly thin. In her fifties, she still moved like a young woman.

"Dr. Scott. Stephanie, isn't it? Sit, please." She nodded in the direction of an overstuffed chair, then dropped wearily into the chair behind her desk. "Do you know if Elizabeth Rooney is, in fact, a lesbian?" she said without preamble.

Stephanie sat as she was directed and settled her body deeply into the chair. "I haven't talked with her myself, Judge Cutter. I was called in by Andrew Brown to testify concerning Gregory Rooney. Everything I said about him was true. He does come from a terrible background and —"

"And so does almost everybody else who appears in my court," Judge Cutter said brusquely. Despite her tone, she kept smiling. "Why do you think he wants to be with those two children so much?"

"He says he loves them."

"And beats them half to death in a drunken rage, not once but several times." Alice Cutter looked grimly at her fingernails and frowned. "If he really loved them, he'd get himself into a treatment program. He won't, of course. He really believes himself blameless. Too many people have made excuses for him."

Stephanie responded defensively, "I was not trying to make excuses for him, your honor. His lawyer asked me to do the psychologicals for the case. I guess he simply had no other grounds on

7

which to attempt to accomplish what the man hired him to do and —"

"I know! I know!" Alice Cutter interrupted. "But he was more than willing to take Rooney's money even though he knew there wasn't a chance in hell of winning with me hearing the case. Lawyers! Pieces of garbage! Yes, I know I was one myself before I became a judge, but that's no excuse." Suddenly she laughed loudly at herself.

Stephanie retained a serious expression as she slowly expelled her next words. "Judge Cutter, I — there was nothing unethical or illegal about his defense and I don't appreciate —"

"Alice, in here," the judge interrupted again. "Listen, I know even the most lowly scumbag deserves someone to put up a decent defense. Forgive me, and forget my little outburst, will you? Do you think he'll leave them alone now?" She stared into Stephanie's eyes as if searching for something hidden behind them. As if she might find something there that the younger woman might not readily reveal.

"Who knows for sure? It's a truism in the field of psychology that the best predictor of future behavior is past behavior. And he hasn't left them alone since she separated from him. If he gets drunk, he'll get angry again, and she'll most likely be his target."

"That's what I think will happen too." Alice picked up the bud vase and inhaled the rosy fragrance, never taking her eyes from Stephanie's face. "You know, you're a very attractive woman. Pretty. Very pretty."

"Thank you." Stephanie blushed.

"A little thin perhaps. How old are you? Twenty eight? Thirty?"

"Judge Cutter, I don't think —"

"Alice." She silenced her with her hand. "I'm sorry. I want you to do me a personal favor, Stephanie. Talk with Mrs. Rooney and tell her she was lucky this case was tried in front of me. There are other judges in this system, especially some of the men, who would find the mere accusation of lesbianism sufficient cause to award those children to Rooney in spite of what he's done to them in the past."

"Just on his word alone? He didn't even pretend to present any evidence."

"You bet. If he were to get pictures of those two women holding hands, much less doing something really sexual, they'd be back in court and he'd have a good chance of getting the kids. And if he really believes that she *is* a lesbian — God knows what he might do. Men like Rooney wear their masculinity on their sleeves and in their fists. His ego couldn't take her being with a woman."

"I'll do what I can," Stephanie said, forcing a smile.

"Are you a lesbian, Stephanie?"

Stephanie looked decidedly nonplussed, but silently struggled to stay cool. "Would it be any of your business if I were?" she asked stiffly.

Alice Cuter was quiet for a moment. "Even though you and I have never met before today, Stephanie, I've heard quite a lot about you and your work. I know, for example, that you don't usually take cases like this. Rumor has it that you're single.

9

People like to talk, you know. They say you haven't tried to hide the fact that you see a lot of lesbians in your private practice."

"Does that matter?" Stephanie asked acidly. "I treat quite a few schizophrenics too. Does that make me psychotic?"

Alice laughed. "No, certainly not. And personally, it doesn't matter to me one way or another what your sexual persuasion is. I have nothing against lesbians — or schizophrenics either. No, I just thought if you were, you might go a little out of your way to deliver my message to Mrs. Rooney. She seems like a nice person. Will you do it?"

"I told you I'd do what I can. What else can I say?" Stephanie didn't try to hide her aggravation over the personal direction the conversation had taken.

"Don't be offended, Stephanie. A couple of years ago I heard a case very similar to this one, except that the wife made no bones about her lesbianism. Some men go crazy over such a thing. That husband killed them all and then killed himself. He murdered two lovely little girls with a kitchen knife, shot his wife and her lover with a shotgun, then put a pistol in his own mouth. And he was under injunction not to come near *them* too. The law is nearly helpless in such matters, and, too often, the ex-wives refuse to have these men locked up — because of fear, poverty, whatever. I would warn her myself, but somehow it doesn't seem — prudent."

Stephanie unexpectedly felt a warmth for the judge in spite of her curt manner and probing questions. Hers was undoubtedly a trying profession. "I promise I'll talk with her. And I hope you won't think badly of me for testifying in Rooney's defense. I had a hunch after talking with the lawyer what his psychologicals would show. I was confident that my report would do him more harm than good. I even told Andrew Brown that before we came to court."

Alice Cutter smiled and stood up abruptly. "Don't worry, Stephanie. I have only admiration for you. Perhaps we shall meet again. And get to know each other better. I certainly hope so."

"That would be nice, Ju . . . Alice." Stephanie felt a glow of pleasure at the prospect.

Their parting handshake was firm and comfortable.

* * * * *

When the door had closed securely behind Stephanie, Alice Cutter reached for the phone and dialed a familiar number.

"Billie," she said. "It's me. I've just talked with your girl. She's the one we need, all right. I'll set it up when you say so."

She listened for a moment. "She wouldn't admit anything and I just couldn't bring myself to mention Robin Oakley. Something told me that was still a very painful subject."

As she listened to the response from the other end of the line, she toyed with the framed picture of three small children that sat on her desk. Suddenly she smiled broadly. "No, Billie. I did *not* try to charm her. Besides, she wouldn't be attracted to me. I'm much too old for her."

And after a few seconds, "Yes, I've heard youth

is a state of mind, but you're too old for her too. I'll get her there my own way. Don't worry!"

Then finally, "I hope it will be soon. I really miss you."

When she hung up she felt happier than she had in days.

* * * * *

The midday sun had raised tiny bubbles on the surface of the tar-covered parking lot by the time Stephanie headed across it in the direction of her dark blue Cutlass. The summer air smelled faintly sweet, like licorice candy. Tall lilac bushes, in full bloom, framed the lot and muted the noise from the heavy Broad Street traffic.

Stephanie searched through her purse as she walked. Usually she made a habit of storing her car keys carefully away in the side pocket of her bag. Now they were missing. She was absolutely sure she had put them there after she locked the car. Her growing irritation threatened to overshadow the good feeling her conversation with Alice Cutter had given her. Where were those damned keys? Dammit! Where were they? She had to get back to the office.

She was vaguely aware of a nearby ambulance siren. Then she heard another sound. Breathing. Shallow, harsh breathing. She smelled him before she saw him. The odor of his cheap after-shave made her glance up from her search. Then she recognized the whine of his voice.

"Here, Doc. Looking for these?" The car keys dangled from Greg Rooney's middle finger. His face was cut with a sly grin.

12

Stephanie struggled not to back away from him. She held her hand out, palm up. "Give me those keys, Mr. Rooney. I have a one o'clock appointment. I don't have time to fool around with you."

"Fool around? That what you want? You're a corker, ain't you, Doc? What makes you think I'd want to fool around with you? I just found your keys for ya. Guess you dropped 'em. Like to talk to you though." He laid the keys on her palm, then caressed her smooth flesh suggestively with the tips of his fingers before he turned them loose.

"You'll have to call my office and make an appointment if you have anything to say to me." She looked around the parking lot. The court building was surrounded by busy streets, but no one was in sight. No one could see them from the street because of the bushes. She was virtually alone with Rooney. Instantly, her heart throbbed hard in the hollow of her throat and a tiny stream of sweat poured hot between her breasts.

Stephanie wrapped her left hand around the handle of the car door, hoping against hope that she might have forgotten to lock it, but Rooney was too quick. He circled her hand with his own and pushed her hard against the door before she could get the key in the lock.

She turned her head to look back at him, and found her eyes at the same level as his grinning mouth. He cloying smell of bourbon and the sour stench of his sweat almost took her breath away. She felt him move himself against her buttocks, then felt his penis grow. He had her pinned tight to the car.

"Please, Mr. Rooney, don't do this. It won't

improve your case. You need help. Let me find a therapist who can help you."

"Fuck you," he muttered, then laughed derisively and ran his hand lightly down her thigh. "You save your help for the loonies who need it, smart lady. I don't need none of your goddamned shrink talk. You can feel *that,* can't you? That's all a man needs."

He pushed himself harder against her, forcing her body to press against the steaming hot car. Her breasts burned as if someone was squeezing them too hard. A scream welled up in her throat, then caught, swelling up inside her until she thought her chest might explode.

Intuitively, she knew her fear would only excite him more. She told herself to ignore the pain, to control the panic. Finally she was able to speak. "All right. What do you want, Mr. Rooney?"

His words slurred thickly as he spoke, but he eased back away from her slightly. "Name's Greg, doll. Greg. And I told you what I want. I want my fucking wife and kids back. They're mine, you hear? You tell that dyke of a judge there ain't nothing wrong with me. Got a little drunk, that's all. You tell her."

She could hear his breath pumping in and out just above her ear. She looked back over her shoulder again. His eyes were shut tight. And he was smiling. Then she understood the bastard was getting off on what he was doing to her.

She took a small step backward, then another, pushing herself away from the hot car. His response was a muffled sort of groan, but he gripped the hand on the door tighter.

"Mr. Rooney, you let me go. You don't want to

get into more trouble. Just let me go and I promise I won't tell anyone that this happened."

His eyes blinked open. "Name's Greg, I told ya. And it don't work that way, doll. You'll promise anything to get away from me — just like my ol' lady does. But you'll tell. *If* there was anything to tell, that is. I ain't done nothing to you. Yet. And I won't if you promise to get me my kids back."

"Mr. Rooney — Greg — let me go. The judge has made her decision. I can't do anything more. Let me go. Please."

He giggled and forced his knee in between her legs. "Please," he mocked her. "Ple-e-ase. You begging for me to give it to you? I'll be happy to give it to you, you little whore."

"Greg —"

"Shut up, bitch!" he shouted angrily in her ear. Suddenly he was panting. With his free hand he grabbed at her crotch. "You told lies about me in the court. You told that fuckin' judge I was a psychopath! I heard you! Well, I ain't no psycho! I'm as sane as the next one and I'm gonna take you somewhere and show you!"

Icy fear filled her stomach and flowed down her legs until she thought she might fall. She had to do something besides talk — and quick. She remembered the keys clutched in her right hand. Bright flashes of light leaped in front of her eyes. Momentarily she felt faint. If she missed him, if she only made him mad by trying to resist him, he might kill her. Then her strength came to her in a rush.

Without turning, she struck backward with the keys. Hard.

As she raked downward across his face, he screamed and sprayed her with saliva. He moved backward suddenly, then stumbled, sitting down hard on the sticky pavement.

She saw his mouth open in a wail. The look on his face was so horrid, so full of hatred, it made her knees buckle and she almost fell herself. She clutched again at the car door to steady herself, then forced the key into the door lock.

The engine caught on the first try and she rammed the gear shift hard into drive. The car jumped the curb and left a trail of rubber on the street. She looked back briefly before turning in front of the courthouse. Rooney was holding his head in his hands and there was a growing circle of blood collecting on his shirt.

Thirty minutes later Stephanie pulled into the safety of her office driveway and put her head in her hands and wept. For the first time in her life, she had knowingly hurt another human being. And even though she knew she had done no more to Rooney than he deserved, she felt more ashamed than she thought was possible.

CHAPTER TWO

Months earlier, Robin Oakley had read in the *Reader's Digest* — which she faithfully consumed cover to cover each month — that watching a tank full of fish was a very effective stress reducer. And Robin had believed that her lover, Stephanie Scott, was in dire need of some way to reduce her stress. They had argued almost daily about something or other for more than a year.

It aggravated Stephanie that Robin was so willing to take the *Digest*'s pronouncements as the truths of the universe. She insisted there wasn't any scientific evidence that fish watching was good for anything. But, in the long run, her logic hadn't stopped Robin from buying a terribly expensive, hundred-gallon tank and installing it in the den. Then she had spent even more money to have a man from the pet store spend hours carefully and artfully installing colored rock, filters, heaters, plants, and finally, fish — an exquisite, breathtaking collection of tropical fish.

"I will not watch those stupid things! They bite each other's tails off and eat their own babies!" Stephanie had told Robin indignantly. "If you want to waste your money, you waste it, but what's wrong between us is not going to be resolved by guppies."

"Stephie, if you were just half as willing to work on *our* problems as you are to help your clients with theirs —"

"*We* don't have a problem, Robin! How many times do I have to tell you? It's your *job* that's the problem! It makes you — I don't know — different. You put on that damned uniform and I swear you — you swagger. And you drink too much when you go out with those gun-happy jocks you work with! You know my attitude toward your being a policewoman. I hate it! Fish can't change that!"

Robin had finally gotten enough of her attitude and left her, but she knew Stephanie had been partially right. Mere fish could never have stopped the personal problems that bloomed like storm clouds between them. Possibly nothing could have — their differences were so fundamental.

Now, without Robin, Stephanie had learned to appreciate the spectacular color-shows the fish tirelessly put on. Caring for them took up some of the time she found on her hands. And when she fed them or cleaned their tank, she watched, and succumbed to their hypnotic beauty. It became a ritual to sit before the tank with the den lights off each day after dinner, watching the fish. Sometimes even talking to them. Sometimes crying. Sometimes merely meditating.

Some days, the troublesome days like this one had been, her mind drifted back to the good times when Robin was still around; to the times when they made love in the late afternoons; to the times when things had not yet gone haywire between them. Robin always seemed to be sexually wired after a really rough day on the job, ready to release the tension, ready to channel the workaday frustrations into shared passion.

From the moment they had first made love, it was Robin who was the sexual leader, the one who knew exactly what to do and when. Robin was the one who took Stephanie to heights she had never forgotten and never dreamed of reaching again. Even now, she felt the wetness begin, stimulated by the unsummoned memories. Without thinking about what she was doing, she pressed the dampness with her fingers.

Stephanie softly cursed the phone when it rang. The jangling noise pushed away the sought-after tranquility as surely as if an electric shock had been delivered to her body.

She moved to the other end of the brushed corduroy sofa and grabbed the phone just before the answering machine picked up. "Dr. Scott here."

"Hello, Stephie."

Quick pain stabbed her chest, and her body

seemed to turn to jelly at the sound of the familiar voice. She bit hard on her lip until she thought she was in command of herself again. "Robin?"

"I tried to reach you at the office, but Mrs. Bateson said you were in court. I hope I'm not disturbing anything important."

Stephanie forced a light tone into her voice. "Just me and the fish. Well, now that you mention it, I was about to crawl in bed with that new woman who plays on *Dallas,* but I guess she can wait."

"Sounds interesting. And more than a little sarcastic, too."

"Yes, I guess it was. Sorry." Then before she could stop herself, she blurted, "How's your new friend?"

"Actually, it's her I'm calling about. Steph, I need a favor. Could you possibly come over here? I've got a problem. Rather, Megan's got a problem and I wondered if you would talk to her."

Stephanie shook her head in disbelief. How could Robin ask her to come to the aid of the new woman in her life? Without emotion she said, "I'm flattered that you thought of me, Robin. I assumed you had forgotten me altogether since I haven't heard from you in so long, but I really don't think I'm the one to help your girlfriend."

"I'm at my wits' end," Robin said lamely. "I know it takes a lot of nerve to ask you to do this, Steph, but I know what a good therapist you are. I trust you."

"There are a lot of good therapists in Richmond. I think you should find somebody who can be more — detached. Besides, I'm not taking on any new clients."

In the silence that followed, Stephanie became aware of the pounding of her heart and the sick feeling lying heavy in the pit of her stomach. She closed her eyes and imagined Robin's face. It was an intelligent face and a kind face as well; the face of a woman capable of great tenderness and compassion. She regretted her sharp retort.

"We — she doesn't need someone to take her on as a regular client. Just somebody to talk to tonight. Stephanie, if I knew anybody else to call, I would. I don't mean to sound melodramatic, but she's in pretty bad shape. I need you, Steph. I'm asking you for old times' sake. Will you come?"

Stephanie hesitated, then answered, "I'm sorry, Robin. I didn't mean to be so damned rude. I've just had a bitch of a day myself. Can you tell me what the problem is?"

"This is awkward and it's too complicated to explain over the phone. Can you come here? We'll — I'll pay you for your time."

"Don't be silly. I don't want your money. I'll come — for old times' sake — like you said. Give me an hour."

"Thanks, Steph," Robin said, and hung up before she could change her mind.

Stephanie stared at the phone, trying to regain her composure. Something must be very wrong for Robin to call. They hadn't spoken to each other for over six months.

* * * * *

She almost ignored the phone the second time it rang. She had just put on her jacket and was

21

reaching for the doorknob. What the hell, she thought, I'll just have to answer the beeper later anyway. She went back into the dimly lit den, slipped off an earring and lifted the phone.

"Dr. Scott here," she said impatiently.

"Doc, this here's Rooney. I jus' wanted to tell you how sorry I am about this afternoon an' to let you know you didn't hurt me bad. I know you wouldn't want to hurt me, now would you?" His words were slurred.

Stephanie let her breath out in a soft hiss. All she needed was another round with Rooney.

"Good, Mr. Rooney. I'm glad you're okay, but I have to hang up now. I was just on my way out."

"Wait, Doc. I have somethin' to tell you. You'll want to hear this. Doc, I've had enough of ever'body's shit, you hear me?"

"You're drunk, Rooney. Go somewhere and sleep it off. Then call me back if you think you have something to tell me."

He laughed deep in his throat.

"No, lady. You can't get rid of me that easy. If you don't listen now, I'll come out to your goddamned house. You liked what I gave you this afternoon, didn't you? I'll give you some more if you don't listen. You hear?"

Stephanie said nothing for fear that her voice might tremble. The events of the day had affected her profoundly.

"You listen!" Rooney screamed. "You fucking women! You bitches! You got no respect for a man. You tell that damned queer wife of mine that I ain't

22

through with her yet. She can't fuck me over this way. Those kids are mine. The house is mine. And she's mine. You tell her that!"

"Mr. Rooney, you are a very sick man and you've had too much to drink. In the shape you're in, you can only hurt your children. Leave them alone. And get some help." Her calm tone was measured.

"Goddamned gold-diggin' whores. All of you! You fucked up know-it-all shrink and that whore of a judge. You're all going to pay for this! You tell 'em all. I ain't finished with any of you. I'll get you all for this!"

"I'm going to hang up now, Mr. Rooney, and if you ever call me again, I'm going to call the police and have you arrested. Understand?

She didn't wait for an answer before she dropped the phone back in its cradle, picked up her purse and headed for the door. At that moment, she wanted to be with Robin more than anything in the world.

* * * * *

It was a little after eight-thirty when Stephanie turned into Robin's driveway. The house was large. Much larger than her own. A sleek white Cadillac sat on one side of the drive and next to it, an aging red convertible. Seeing the 1972 Pontiac GTO that Robin had babied and loved so much made her feel light-headed. The last time she had seen the car up close was the night she had watched tearfully from the window while Robin pitched the bulk of her wardrobe into the back seat. When she finally drove away, Stephanie had hurried to the bathroom and thrown up violently.

As she went up the front walk Stephanie drew the evening air deep into her lungs to steady herself. A dog barked behind the closed door as she lifted her hand to knock. She wiped the sweat from her palms on her slacks, then tugged at her pullover as she waited. A small voice far inside her head whispered, almost too soft for her to hear: *You're not up to this, are you? You still have time to run away if you want to.*

No, she really didn't want to run away from this. Sooner or later she would have to face the fact that Robin had found someone new. Perhaps she was someone who would be more understanding, if not someone who could love her more. But no one could do that, she was sure.

Robin took a long time to answer. When she opened the door, she stood silent for a moment behind the screen, then said quietly, "Thank you for coming, Steph. Come in." In her arms, a tiny black poodle wiggled and licked her tongue in Stephanie's direction.

Stephanie shivered as she stepped through the doorway. The air-conditioned house immediately seemed too cool to her warm body and she hugged herself.

"Hi, Oodles. How've you been, baby?" Stephanie said to the squirming animal and reached to take her from Robin. Oodles had been their dog. They had gotten her when she was barely six weeks old.

The tension in Robin's rigid shoulders betrayed her own uneasiness as she handed over the dog. She was watching Stephanie intently, but when she met her eyes, she smiled nervously and looked away.

Robin's one-sided smile was even sweeter than Stephanie had remembered. Her cropped blonde hair lay tight against her head, except where it curled down over her forehead and ears. She was neither beautiful nor ugly, this woman she still loved. Yet her looks were enormously appealing, her blue eyes capable of conveying gentleness and sensitivity. When she and Robin had met five years ago at a University of Richmond symposium Stephanie had given entitled "Forensic Psychology and Law Enforcement," it had been those amazing, expressive eyes that had attracted her so. And it had been those same eyes that had finally drawn her into Robin's bed and into her first lesbian love affair. Now, Robin looked unchanged. So much the same. Stephanie longed to kiss her, or hold her close at least. Her face flushed hot in spite of the coolness of the house. She knew she could not afford to dwell on the old memories. She kissed the dog's black nose, making a too-loud smacking sound.

Robin reached out awkwardly to pat the poodle's head. She met Stephanie's eyes again and winked shyly.

Stephanie stiffened. Without warning, she saw herself as she must look to Robin. Too thin. Too tired. And too needy.

"You look beautiful," Robin said, as if reading her thoughts.

Stephanie's throat tightened. Only when she had settled herself on the elaborate brocade sofa did she dare reply. "Please, Robin, don't say things like that. Let's stick to the business I came here for."

Robin shook her head in apology, then crossed to a nearby easy chair. Carefully, she eased her usually lithe, athletic body down and stretched her right leg straight out in front of her on a small footstool.

"As you can see, I'm not up to my usual self. But it's beginning to heal."

"Oh, my Lord, what have you done to yourself?"

"Just a scratch, really. A juvie with a Saturday night special decided he didn't want me to arrest him for holding up a liquor store a couple weeks ago. Just a little guy, twelve years old. I didn't believe he'd shoot me. Took a bullet in the calf. Didn't amount to much, but the department put me on leave for a while. I'll be as good as new before long."

"If I had known . . ." Stephanie looked at Robin with a pained expression. The fear that something like this — or worse — would happen had been the main thing that had come between them. Stephanie had hated watching her leave in the mornings, wondering if she would come home that night. She had begged her to leave police work for something else — anything else that was safer.

"I know you always told me it was a matter of time," Robin said, again as if reading her mind. "And you were right, of course, but I still don't want to do anything else with my life. Doing police work is my karma or something, Steph. I'll be more careful from here on out though. Not that I might not . . ."

Stephanie stopped her with a wave of her hand and clamped her teeth together tight to stop herself from finishing the thought. *Get yourself killed or kill someone else.* She put her hand up to her temple

26

and rubbed hard. The conversation was too familiar. Too much like some old recurring nightmare. Had Megan and Robin had the same disagreement? She could have wept on the spot. Instead she petted the dog who had settled herself comfortably on her lap.

"You wanted to see me — something about Megan," Stephanie said thickly. "You want me to talk to her?"

Robin twisted her ear before she spoke. It was an old gesture that meant she was unsure how to proceed. "She promised she would talk to you, Steph, but she took a sleeping pill and went to bed. Stephie, something strange happened to her while I was in the hospital. She got a phone call from a man that scared the bejesus out of her. It wasn't your usual hot-breathed obscenities call. This guy asked her if she was Megan Cameron from Winston-Salem, North Carolina. She thought maybe it was some old schoolmate of hers, so she told him she used to live in Winston-Salem and her parents still live there. She said he laughed and asked if she had had a birthmark on her . . . her right breast removed or if it still looked like a red heart." Robin shifted uneasily in her chair and rubbed through her jeans at her injured leg.

"You . . ." Stephanie broke off, surprised at the intimate references, but she recovered quickly. "I guess it's safe to assume she has such a birthmark. How would a stranger have known about that? If the man *was* a stranger."

"That's just the point," Robin said, blushing slightly. "Meg says that she has never . . . never slept with a man. Hasn't had a male lover. And I believe her. Why would she lie about that?"

Stephanie shrugged. She knew very little about Megan. She would just as soon keep it that way. She stared at her shoes and said nothing.

"But what she did tell me that she hadn't told me before was that she was raped while she was still in high school. The man stripped all her clothes off and made pictures of her before he raped her. And they never caught him."

"And she's afraid this might be the same man."

"Precisely. She's sure it's him."

"Robin, you know this is a matter for the police. Not for a psychologist. Call one of your buddies from headquarters."

"I did. Right after it happened. You think I'm crazy, I guess, but Meg is just torn all to pieces by this. She's scared. She won't eat. Can't sleep. I got her to see her regular doctor. He gave her tranquilizers and sleeping pills, but she needs to talk to somebody about this, Steph. It's raised all kinds of stuff that she needs to deal with."

"I can refer her."

"Stephie, she won't see anyone else. I've begged her. She feels guilty or something. She finally agreed to talk to you tonight — just talk. Then she got more and more upset the closer the time came for you to get here. So," she added apologetically, "she went to bed. I tried to call you back but you'd already left. She's spending most of her time in bed now."

Stephanie sat silent for a full two minutes, debating with herself. Then she stood up. "I shouldn't do this, Robin. I'm much too . . . too close to this situation because of our past relationship. It's not exactly unethical for me to see Megan, it's just not wise. And I'll probably regret it, but if you can get her to call the office — or you call — I'll see her. Make an appointment. Then force her to come if you have to. I know you won't see it this way, but right now you're being much too patient with her and much too kind." She smiled at her for the first time since she arrived. "Maybe you were too patient with me too — until I finally pushed you too far."

Robin didn't answer her, but the look in her eyes said it all. It was the first time Stephanie had admitted to any responsibility for their breakup.

"Goodbye, Robin," she said. "Take good care of Oodles."

* * * * *

Megan Cameron moaned loudly and woke herself up. She had gone to sleep under a starched white sheet which now lay at the foot of the bed, crumpled into a wrinkled ball. She awoke in another place — in the dimness of the back of her closet underneath the row of blouses which were arranged neatly according to color. Purple shades to the left, followed by blues, green, yellows, oranges and pink-reds. She had learned about the order of the visual spectrum in high school Biology class and it was comforting to know that even her clothes obeyed the natural law of the universe. She liked that. Order was important.

She couldn't remember leaving the comfort of the cool sheets, but was not particularly surprised to find herself in the closet, curled into the fetal position. It was not the first time she had awakened in a strange place. Nor did she expect it to be the last.

Somnambulism, the doctors had said, was not a particularly hazardous affliction. Sleepwalkers rarely did anything dangerous, like walking on ledges or crossing heavy traffic. Contrary to popular belief, they almost never left the safety of their own familiar houses. And besides, at the first hint of danger, something deep in the protective part of the brain snapped them right back into wakefulness.

Megan had learned that the really bad part about being a somnambulist was that it was sometimes embarrassing. More often, it was plain uncomfortable to sleep in a place not designed for sleeping. Megan crawled on hands and knees from the closet and pulled herself up on the side of the bed. She rubbed the back of her neck and then the calves of her legs. Her shoulders and legs were cramped from lack of circulation.

Her nylon gown was soaked with sweat. She stripped it off. In the mirror, she appraised her naked body and liked what she saw. She was thin in the places she thought she should be, but with full breasts and buttocks. She never exercised, as she considered the expenditure of energy a waste, but she took care not to eat or drink too much and did not hesitate to fast for days if she found her weight not to her liking. With admiration, she weighed her breasts in her hands, pushing them up and out.

She was smiling at her reflection when Robin appeared behind her.

"Hi," Robin said to the mirror Megan.

"Hello, golden girl," Megan said to her in a sexy voice, but she didn't take her eyes off her own body.

Robin's heart speeded up and she felt instantly as if her rib cage were being squeezed in a vise. Megan's physical beauty always took her breath away. "I thought I heard a noise. Are you all right?" Robin asked.

"I'd be better if you were beside me." She stretched her body in feline fashion, then sat down on the bed and patted a spot beside her.

"I thought I heard you groaning."

"I was having a dream."

"About what? It must have been a bad one. You sounded — funny."

"A good one. About you." She leaned back, spread her legs slightly, and motioned to Robin. "You can have me."

That was what Megan always said: "You can have me." Not I love you. Or even I want you. Not once in the weeks they had been together had she told Robin that she loved her. Instead, she gave her masses of flowers and gifts, smothering her with extravagance and overwhelming her with generosity. And of course, she gave her her body.

"Meg . . ."

"It makes you angry that I won't say I love you, doesn't it?"

"No. It hurts — a lot."

"I guess I'm different from you," Megan said, parting her legs a little more. "But I've told you I can't say that. It doesn't matter. My body belongs to you anyway. I'll show you if you'll come here."

Sex had been easy for them from the start. So easy that Robin sometimes felt herself smothered by the passion. But she longed for love along with the sex. She needed to be someone's great love. Once she had thought she would be Stephanie's.

Megan was looking at her, her soft lips parted, her eyes searching Robin's face for a response. She wet her lips suggestively with her tongue.

Robin moved toward the bed. For reasons she could not define, she felt cold.

"Rub my back?" Megan asked and flipped onto her stomach without waiting for a reply.

Robin sat on the bed and began kneading the skin of her back and buttocks. For a few seconds, everything seemed normal. Then, without warning, a tremor ran through Megan's body and she flung herself violently off the bed and onto the floor. Her face flushed red as she got to her feet and her expression was pure rage.

Robin rose, startled, and moved toward her. "Honey, what's wrong?"

Megan's eyes were wild and glazed. She began to shout with such energy that she sprayed Robin with spit. "You bitch! You goddamned bitch! You let that shithead do it again! Why do you let him do it?"

Robin's eyes grew wide. The voice wasn't Megan's. It was a voice she had never heard before. Megan's body was stiff and straight, her hands balled into fists at her sides.

"Megan?"

"Don't 'Megan' me, you stinking bitch!" She waved her arms at something she seemed to see in the air.

For several moments, Megan continued to shout obscenities at the top of her lungs. Robin grabbed her arms and tried to soothe her while Megan wailed and stared off into infinity.

At last, when she calmed a little, Robin took her by the shoulders and shook her, trying to force her to make eye contact. "Megan, can you see me?" She was sure Megan had slipped into some kind of trance.

"Of course, you bitch. And I hate you!"

"Who are you talking to, Megan? It's Robin. You don't hate me."

"No! You're not her! You're trying to fool me, but I know you. And you let him do it!"

"Who am I then, if I'm not Robin?"

"Her!"

With that she jerked away, turned, tripped over the wastebasket, and fell with a crash. On the floor she drew her knees up to her chest and clutched at herself as if she were in horrible pain. She groaned softly.

Robin knelt beside her and took her hand, begged her to be calm. When she did relax a little, Robin lifted her back onto the bed and pinned her arms down beside her.

Finally, Megan blinked and her eyes focused on Robin's face. "What are you doing?"

"Trying to help you."

"Help me do what?"

"You don't remember any of that? What just happened. What you said."

"You were about to rub my back."

Unsure what to do next, Robin swallowed hard, and tried to force out words that were refusing to come. Had Megan been reliving some kind of trauma or what? She silently resolved to be sure she made an appointment with Stephanie.

Weakly Robin whispered, "Sure, hon, roll over."

Within moments, Megan slept soundly.

CHAPTER THREE

It was a week before Megan Cameron called for an appointment and, coincidentally, Stephanie heard from Alice Cutter again the same day. She had just poured herself a cup of coffee when the intercom buzzed.

"Yes, Annie. Is Mr. Cotton here already? He's early."

"No, Dr. Scott, a Judge Cutter is on the phone. Something about a case she's hearing. Shall I put her through?"

"Yes, I'll take the call." She was pleased. She

found Alice attractive. And God knew she needed a distraction from her obsessive thoughts about Robin. She pushed the blinking phone button. "Stephanie Scott."

"Alice Cutter, Stephanie. I know you're busy and I'm sorry to call you at your office, but I've got a case coming up tomorrow that I need an expert opinion on. I wondered if you could stop by the jail this evening and take a look at this fellow. I've got to decide tomorrow whether to let him go or ship him to the state hospital."

Stephanie smiled, wondering about Alice Cutter's motives. Her request was unusual. Was it possible that the good judge had a personal interest in her? "Do you have an assessment from Mental Health yet?"

"Yes, I do. But to tell you the truth . . ." She could hear Alice light a cigarette and take a deep drag. "To tell you the truth, they sent this new fellow up here who wasn't dry behind the ears, some kind of psychiatric social work intern or something, and I can't make heads or tails out of his report. I don't honestly think he knows his ass . . . well, we sometimes ask for another opinion in a sensitive case anyway. We'll pay you for your time, of course."

"What time could I see him?"

"If six o'clock tonight would suit you, I thought I could meet you at the jail, then maybe we could have dinner together. What do you think?"

Stephanie looked at her watch. Four o'clock already. Two more patients. Thank God it was Friday. Besides, she wanted to see Alice Cutter again. "I can make it by six-thirty."

"Good."

Slowly she sank into the wingback chair behind her desk. She closed her eyes. Alice Cutter, you are up to something. And I wonder if I know what it is.

* * * * *

Later that evening at City Hall, Stephanie gazed around the conference room in which she had unexpectedly found herself. The walls were lined with yellowing portraits of the city's ancient greats: Robert E. Lee, J.E.B. Stuart, Jefferson Davis. Red leather-backed chairs were set evenly around a long oval table. The floor was covered with a faded pinkish carpet that needed replacing.

She deliberately avoided making eye contact with the two men who sat across the table from her. They had been introduced by Alice Cutter as Dr. Fred MacIntosh and Dr. Jason Jefferies, both scientists from Virginia Commonwealth University. Jefferies had seemed pleasant enough, but Fred MacIntosh barely grunted a strained greeting before plastering a childlike pout across his face and lapsing into an uncomfortable silence.

Beyond the terse introductions, Alice had said only that the meeting was of extreme importance to the community and to her personally and that she begged their indulgence until another person could get there.

Stephanie felt disappointed and moderately irritated. Even betrayed. By Alice Cutter. She also felt a little silly for letting herself believe that Alice was attracted to her. Hadn't she read in the papers that she was a widow with grown children?

When the other person finally arrived, he

37

slammed the door noisily behind him. He gave the instant impression of a man who was used to coming in late to meetings that could not start without him. An important man who habitually arrived later just for the effect it provided. He offered no apologies as he sat down at the head of the table and opened a thick file folder.

"How are you, Alice?" Black eyes glittered as he spoke, but his face was otherwise without expression. He made no move to shake her hand.

"Fine. Just fine, Phillip."

"My name is Phillip King," he stated matter-of-factly to the others. His body language said that the name carried weight in some circles. He straightened the carefully knotted tie that was perfectly coordinated with his gray suit. A lock of dark hair fell in little-boy fashion over his high forehead. In a few years he would have a prominent widow's peak.

Stephanie glanced at Alice Cutter, who, at the moment, was keeping her eyes focused on the table. She cleared her throat to get her attention, then cleared it again, but Alice seemed not to have heard.

"For the benefit of those of you who were brought here under false pretenses — you, Dr. Scott, and you, Dr. MacIntosh — I am an associate of the Federal Bureau of Investigation. The others know who I am. You must believe me that it was necessary you not know in advance that this meeting was to occur. Try not to be . . . upset by whatever deception was used to get you here."

MacIntosh squirmed uneasily in his chair and shot a puzzled look at Jefferies. She wondered what kind of cock-and-bull story he had been told in order to get him here.

In spite of the apparent clandestine nature of the meeting, the windows were wide open. Thanks to daylight saving time, the sky was still bright and warm. A breeze carried in the slight smell of roses from the courthouse lawn. Jefferies stared at a robin that was working hard to extract a long worm from the grass.

King continued in staccato fashion. "I am associated with a branch of the agency sometimes referred to as the Arm. Our job is to recruit regular citizens as temporary operatives. We ask people such as yourselves to aid their government by helping us infiltrate certain organizations which cannot be approached by our professionals. My purpose today is to solicit your cooperation.

"Outside of your fair Virginia city, there is a so-called commune which is headed by a man named Dexter Spencer. Mr. Spencer claims that the commune is a religious order of sorts. That makes it a perfectly legal endeavor here in our home of the brave and the free, and it even enjoys tax-exempt status. Mr. Spencer also claims that his group has no political leanings. We have reason to believe otherwise, although we have not been able to substantiate that." He paused as he pulled a ring of keys out of his jacket pocket. He flipped them from one palm to the other a few times before he went on.

"You people have been selected by the Arm for very good reasons. One, each of you has some prominence in the community so you would be known to Spencer. No one who is a stranger to him has yet to be admitted. Others from your community have already joined him as recruits, or perhaps I should say converts. You may even be surprised to find out who some of them are.

"Two, each of you is single with either no children or with grown children. That gives you a certain freedom of movement some others might not have." As King spoke he lovingly caressed the individual keys on the ring.

Stephanie felt her shoulders cramp. She leaned forward, cupping her chin in her hand to relieve some of the tension. She started to speak, but King held up his open palm to stop her. "You will get a chance to ask questions later. If you will, let me finish. There is a third reason you have been selected. Each of you is known to the Arm as a person whose particular skills are needed for this assignment. You are, respectively, an analytic chemist, a lawyer, a psychologist and a geologist. Just why these skills are important will become obvious to you later, should you choose to volunteer for this . . . assignment. Trust me about this. You are capable of doing what the Arm will ask of you. Basically, we want you to associate yourselves with Mr. Spencer's operation, and once you have done this, to gather certain information, the nature of which will be withheld until you have chosen to join us." He ended his speech abruptly and raised his eyebrows, apparently ready for questions.

"Mr. King," Stephanie began. "This whole thing — assignment — whatever, sounds like something for some kind of Mission Impossible Task Force, not a group of lay people. Besides, I have a practice to run. I can't just go gallivanting off to the countryside to join some commune. These other people no doubt have responsibilities as well. Surely you don't expect us to —"

"Dr. Scott, you are quite right," King interjected. "We will not ask you to leave your practice for any protracted period of time. At first, you will just make the contact, visit the commune, find out what we ask you to. If it looks like you need to do more later, then we can make paid arrangements for a vacation from your practice which will allow you to meet our requirements."

Fred MacIntosh spoke next. He had the pallid, almost anemic look of an academic geologist who had never spent a moment working on a field assignment. "Sir, I share Dr. Scott's concern. My research at the university . . ."

"Is funded by the government, Dr. MacIntosh, and we can make any kind of arrangement for you that may be needed. We already pay most of your salary, sir."

MacIntosh blushed, and he clamped his thin mouth tight. His job depended on government grants. He most certainly would be dismissed from the university if the funding for his research were to dry up. MacIntosh realized that he had no option but to do what the dark-eyed man was asking.

Stephanie was outraged. His words to MacIntosh amounted to blackmail. The man probably used such tactics to manipulate people all the time. She searched the face of the other man at the table, Jefferies the chemist, and found it without expression. Stephanie guessed that he had brought MacIntosh in, as Alice Cutter had lured her here.

Possibly he and Cutter had been approached first by King, then had helped select the other two. She looked again at the judge. Alice lifted her head this time and smiled apologetically.

Again Stephanie faced King. "Are we all to assume, Mr. King, that we really have no choice in this matter? That there is some kind of veiled blackmail going on here?"

"Blackmail?" King laughed, then feigned innocence. "No. There are always choices, Dr. Scott. And there are always consequences of our choices. In spite of the fact that we humans like to think we have free will, it is, after all, the outcomes of our choices that control our behavior. What happens as the result of our decisions is what's important to people. Consequences control us just as surely as if we were robots. There is little true freedom for any of us, would you not agree, Dr. Scott? You have, of course, read Dr. Skinner's famous book *Beyond Freedom and Dignity,* where he argues just that point."

Stephanie frowned, but said nothing more. King was blackmailing MacIntosh with no compunction. She wondered what he thought he had on her. Surely he didn't plan to use her lesbianism as a threat. She was out to everyone who mattered. Perhaps he planned to call each of her patients individually and inform them of her sexual preference. Beyond that, she could think of nothing he might try to use to control her, and even that would hardly destroy her practice.

"Besides, Dr. Scott," King continued, "I believe it is true that communes are no novelty to you. Am I not correct?"

Stephanie instantly felt hot and cold in the pit of her stomach. It was a fact that she had been raised in a commune, one called Walden Two after B.F. Skinner's novel about utopian society. It had been located in a tiny community in the foothills of Virginia. King must know all about her if he knew about Walden Two. The only person in Richmond she had told about her background was Robin Oakley. What the hell was really going on here?

King read the concern on Stephanie's face, then settled back in his chair, apparently pleased with the effects his words had had on her. "There is one final factor you all may wish to enter into the equation as you consider your choice. The Arm has reason to believe each of you is on Dexter Spencer's list of future recruits. And it appears that Mr. Spencer only recruits people he has some special use for. There is also evidence that he has some special . . . method for gaining cooperation from people he wishes to make use of, although at the moment we have no idea what it is. Perhaps it would be better to work for the Arm, no matter how reluctant you might feel about doing so, than to be subject to some manipulation of Spencer's. Now, if that is all —" King gathered up his papers.

Fred MacIntosh and Stephanie stared at each other, dumbfounded. King was smiling. "I will be on my way. You have the weekend to consider what I have said. Someone will contact you on Monday for your final answer. I thank you all." And with that he rose and disappeared through the doorway.

Stephanie felt as if she had barely managed to survive something awful, like a jump from an airplane. It was several minutes before she realized that Alice Cutter had reached across the table and put her hand gently on her arm.

"You promised to have dinner with me. Is it still on or are you so angry with me you want to call it off?"

Stephanie rose unsteadily, extracting herself from Alice's touch. Where the room had once felt light and airy, it now seemed heavy and thick. The rose fragrance had turned sickeningly sweet. She felt tears of disappointment threaten to form as she looked steadily at Alice.

"Frankly, I don't know what to think — or feel. But I do believe you owe me some explanation, Alice. And I suppose," she said, letting her breath out slowly, "that dinner is as good a place as any for you to give me some answers."

Alice smiled again and winked. "I know just the place."

* * * * *

Shortly after King's meeting ended, Dexter Spencer began conducting a meeting of his own. To his right sat D. Worthington French, president and principal stockholder of Atlas Chemicals International. Like Phillip King, French never arrived at a meeting on time and had kept Spencer's assembly waiting until seven-fifteen, confident that they would not begin without him. He hustled into the room, radiating authority, set his briefcase on the long table and popped the catches loudly. Only then did he fold his lanky body into the chair reserved for him.

Atlas Chemicals was the east coast's largest

producer of psychoactive drugs and routinely awarded contracts to private laboratories and universities. Consequently, French sat on the boards of a number of Richmond's largest organizations. He assumed Spencer had invited him to this meeting as a potential board member for the commune.

Odell Munsington had arrived ten minutes early for the meeting. That was typical of him as well, for he suspected that whenever two or more people who knew him got together, they gossiped about him behind his back. And usually they did.

In his middle age, Munsington had been a lean, God-fearing, church-loving, Bible-thumper of the first order. His voice would still be recognized by most of the Sunday morning TV watchers, especially the most faithful of his former followers. But most of them had learned to detest his face when it came to light that half of their monetary contributions to God's work had been spent by Munsington on drugs and fast women — and sometimes young boys as well. The other half of the money had gone for huge houses, and cars that were faster than the women. Since his unfortunate accident, as he liked to call it, since he had lost his prime-time program, his cheeks had grown fat, with great folds of flesh hanging from his jaws, and the once athletic body had sprouted a prominent potbelly. He sat on Spencer's left.

Dexter Spencer himself sat at the head of the gleaming mahogany table. In front of him was an ordinary black telephone and a pitcher filled with water. The room was deeply carpeted in green but sparsely furnished. Rich velvet drapes framed a large, smoke-tinted glass window that overlooked a two-acre lake. Around the lake were groups of people, apparently families out for a late summer afternoon of fun and relaxation.

Two other men sat at the far end of the table, staring out over the lake. They appeared bored and unconcerned about the goings-on inside the room. They were Spencer's henchmen.

"I'm glad you could come, Worth," Spencer said. He reached out to shake the slender man's hand. "You remember Odell Munsington, of course."

"Yes, Dexter, we met some years ago, I believe. Some sort of fund-raiser at the Virginia Museum, wasn't it?" He eyed Munsington somewhat suspiciously, but shook his outstretched hand, which was damp and soft.

Munsington smiled broadly. "Wonderful! Just wonderful!" the former televangelist crowed, as if French had asked about his well-being.

Spencer frowned uneasily at the man's strange response, then ran his hand through the hair at the sides and back of his head, dark hair with the texture of steel wool. His face was covered almost to his high, thin cheekbones with similar stuff. Spencer was six-feet-five, with broad knobby shoulders and narrow hips. He was deeply tanned and his clear eyes were mine-shaft black. Although French and Munsington both wore staid dark suits and tightly knotted ties, Spencer was clad in a loose-fitting robe and leather sandals.

"Let's get on with this meeting," French demanded. "I have other things to do. Besides, we all know what we're here for."

Dexter Spencer stroked his beard affectedly as he began to speak. "Gentlemen, I have asked the two of you to join me today for a presentation. But first of all I must give you some information about our little settlement here. We are called Enlightenment and we are indeed enlightened, for we regularly study the great works of mankind. Not only do we consider the Bible and the Koran to be significant, we study and learn from Freud, Jung, Perls, Rogers and Skinner, to name just a few. We meditate morning and evening so that we may grow spiritually and mentally. Many of our members practice yoga.

"We also care for our bodies. All of our food is organically grown. Fruit which will not thrive in the Virginia climate is grown in hothouses. The bread is baked in sod ovens. We eat no meat. We teach that the body is as important as the mind and spirit. We believe in what is commonly called holistic health."

Worth French squirmed in his chair. "Dexter, see here. I am not interested in whatever kind of —" He searched for a word. "— crap you have going on here. You told me you had a business proposition to make. Get on with it."

"And so I have. Be patient, Worth, I'm getting to that. What I wish you to understand first is that the people you see here at the commune, the people you can view from this window, are individuals seeking something more from their lives. They are all looking for salvation of a sort. They come here in the evenings after work. They come for weekends. They spend their vacations here. Some few have given up everything to live permanently on the grounds. We hope others will make that decision soon."

Munsington slapped the table with an open palm. "And when they've come along that far," he said knowingly, "they give you every earthly possession they have, right?" He knew the scam from his own past experience.

"They do. We need money to operate the place, but that's not the point."

"What's the damned point, Spencer? Can we get on with the business?" French's forehead folded into a sour frown of impatience.

Spencer held up his hand. "This is the point, Worth. The human mind is in many ways just like a computer. It takes in information. Input. And it acts on that information. Output. But what comes out of the computer, and what comes out of the human mind, depends entirely on the CPU. The central processing unit. The inside of the machine. It's the guts of the process. You can't see it. You can't hear it. But it's the most important part."

"Good God, Spencer, are you peddling a new computer? Jesus! My company isn't interested in investing in computers!" French exploded. He started to rise from his chair.

"No, no, Worth. Wait. Please. Hear me out."

"Get on with it then. Quit spouting nonsense. I'm a busy man!"

"Consider this," Spencer said, refusing to be rushed. "Many things can modify the inside of a machine. Even the human machine. You, of all people, should know that, French. The psychoactive drugs your company produces are a prime example. With the right drug, a person could, at least theoretically, exert total control over another human being, right?"

"Theoretically, perhaps," French said. "But there

are no drugs like that. You're talking about modern-day alchemy."

Spencer smiled. "Look out the window, gentlemen, and observe. What you will hear on the speakers in this room is also being broadcast through speakers mounted around the lake. The voice you will hear is my voice."

He reached for the telephone in front of him and spoke several unintelligible sentences. The speakers came to life.

"In five seconds, you will remove all of your clothing and that of your children. Five, four, three, two, one. Now."

Around the lake, men and women obediently rose and began stripping themselves. They picked up babies and small children and took the clothes off them. Then they calmly resumed what they had been doing before the message.

"Jesus Christ! You just told them to do it and they did it? If it can't be a drug, then you must have discovered a way to use mass hypnosis," Munsington cried. He slapped his hands together with glee.

"Not exactly, Odell. Something more effective than hypnosis. You see, it is *not* true that people can be made to do anything under a hypnotic spell. Stage hypnotists frequently get people to act silly because it's part of the fun. It's a con. Unconsciously, nobody wants to make the hypnotist look like a jerk in public. Think of it. You'd get booed out of the place for causing the show to flop. Most of it is the conscious mind cooperating with peer pressure. You use the same technique, Odell, in your revivals and services. Get one person to the altar confessing sins and others are embarrassed not to come too."

Munsington looked offended. "Are you implying that I'm some kind of con man? Why I —"

"Of course you are, you old fart!" Spencer laughed at him. "You know perfectly well how to use that kind of peer pressure. The thing is, the solitary individual mind is much harder to manipulate. For example, if I hypnotized you and told you to murder your mother, you wouldn't pay any attention to the suggestion unless you intended to murder her anyway. Hypnosis has definite and serious limitations as a method of behavioral control."

French raised his hand in protest, then said in a voice that dripped with sarcasm, "Absolutely enchanting, Mr. Spencer. How much did it cost you to get those people to strip? People will do a lot of silly things for money too."

"No, Mr. French, not money." Spencer answered. "Look out the window again." He spoke into the telephone once more.

The speakers barked a command. Outside, the two dozen or so naked men and women stood up, retrieved their children one by one, then without hesitation tossed them into the lake. Some of the older children began to swim, but the infants sank out of sight into the muddy water, even as their parents looked on smiling. One or two of the adults turned their backs on the lake and, apparently unconcerned, went back to where they had been sitting.

French shifted uneasily in his chair. Then he took a deep breath and held it.

Munsington sat frozen to his seat for a few

unsteady heartbeats before he got up and went to the huge window for a better look. His jowls had turned as white as birch bark. He whirled to face Spencer. "You're going to let them kill their babies? You're actually going to let them do that? And they're doing it for money? My God, man, that's against human nature!"

Spencer grinned diabolically. "Yes, but it's not because of money. Don't worry about the babies. Watch."

At that moment, a half dozen wet-suited divers appeared at the surface of the lake. Each of them had an infant or two tucked underneath an arm or slung over a shoulder. Without ado, they came out of the lake, returned the screaming babies, apparently no worse for the dip in the lake, to the appropriate parents and walked away.

Spencer looked pleased with himself. "The children were never in any real danger, friends. Those divers were under water long before these people came to the lake today, but they didn't know that."

"Very clever, Spencer," French said, scowling. "*Now* would you care to tell us what this is all about?"

"Very simply, my dear sir, I have found a substance that will modify the central processing unit of the human brain so that all suggestions and commands given, and I do mean *all*, are obeyed instantly."

French looked thoughtful. "And this commune business? Do you drug them to get them to come here?"

"If I have to, to get the people I want to come

here. The commune is legitimate, though, and most people do come here initially for the very reasons I've outlined. But doesn't it make a nice front for experimentation in behavior control? We have all the subjects we need to test and develop this thing — without any outside interference."

"Jesus Christ!" muttered Munsington.

"Yes, Jesus Christ," Spencer said, "or the Devil himself. That's the kind of power the three of us are going to have before we're through."

CHAPTER FOUR

The conversation between Alice and Stephanie consisted at first of small talk. Stephanie picked at the linguine and clam sauce that Alice had expertly whipped up for their dinner. She hadn't touched the salad or the red wine. Alice Cutter ate with appetite, but in silence.

Alice's huge, rambling house sat on a high cliff overlooking the winding, powerful James River, the sloping river banks studded with stands of pine, maple, and scattered oaks which appeared to be blue, then majestic purple in the settling dusk. The panorama from the dining room window had become breathtaking as distant lights from the city began to wink and twinkle energetically.

As Stephanie's gaze moved up and down the river, she became aware of her own reflection in the glass. She thought she looked older than her thirty years. Her honey-colored hair was pulled back too severely. The tortoise-shell glasses were too large for her face. When had it become too much trouble to wear her contacts, she wondered? Her eyes were a deep, brilliant green, totally lacking the yellowish brown that makes most green eyes run toward hazel, and she had once taken great pride in showing them to their best advantage. Stephanie shook her head.

"Quite a view, don't you think? It's the main reason I bought this house. It's really much too big for one person," Alice said. "I hoped you wouldn't mind eating here. I consider this the best restaurant in town, if I do say so myself. I like my own cooking better than anyone else's. I had hoped you'd like it too."

"I'm sorry, Alice. The scenery is beautiful and the food is excellent. I just don't seem to have much of an appetite. This has not been, well, the kind of day I particularly enjoy."

Alice rose to retrieve a bottle of B & B and two glasses. Without asking, she leaned across the table to pour one for Stephanie. Her smell was clean, like soap, and Stephanie noticed that her hands were large and strong. For a slender woman, she had great presence. Her eyes were blue enough to have been the reflection of the sky itself and her skin was dark, as if deeply tanned by the sun.

"Stephanie, I apologize for . . . the way things have happened. We need to have a serious talk," Alice said, settling herself back down at the table. "I know I put you in an awful situation today. You have every right to be angry. I hope you can forgive me."

"You could have told me. You really didn't have to resort to such dramatic cloak-and-dagger tactics." Her voice sounded edgy although she was trying hard to appear unruffled.

"Oh really!" Alice shot back with raised eyebrows. "You think I could have just told you that Uncle Sam wanted you to go to work for him on some undercover mission and you would come tootling down to the courthouse to play Gretchen Good Citizen?"

Stephanie pursed her lips. "I don't appreciate being deceived. And I especially don't appreciate being blackmailed," she said sharply.

Alice frowned. "I don't think you can blame that one on me. If you have to blame somebody, blame it on J. Edgar Hoover. He's the one who kept secret files on everybody. The FBI and the Arm just can't seem to give that up as their major *modus operandi.* Besides, King won't do a damned thing, even if he did think he had something on you — and he doesn't. He was bluffing. He's not even the agent in charge. He was just brought in to get the cooperation of the people who will be involved. You know how men are when they think they might have to work for a woman."

"He must want me in on this real bad. He obviously went to a lot of trouble to find out about my personal history. I guess he thought he had something on me that would assure my getting involved in this business."

Alice looked at Stephanie with genuine concern. She knew she must choose her words carefully if she was going to win the woman's confidence. "Don't blame King. *I* asked for you to be in on this *business,* as you put it. He didn't pick you. I did."

Stephanie's face showed her surprise. "You? What do you have to do with it?"

"Everything. I'm the one who asked the FBI to investigate Enlightenment — that's the name of the commune, in case you didn't know. I've been trying to find someone of your caliber, with your skills, for some time now. When I saw you at work in court the other day, well, I was sure you were the one."

Leaning forward in her chair, Stephanie asked, "The one to do what?"

Alice was silent for a moment, thinking her own thoughts while the grandfather clock in the living room chimed eight. "I guess you should know everything, so let me give you some background information. On me. Everything you ever wanted to know about Alice Cutter, but were afraid to ask." She laughed at her own attempt at levity.

"I grew up in D.C. My mother was from India. She continued her story in earnest. "My own father was born in Silver Spring, Maryland. His family was quite poor. He thought my mother was beautiful, I guess, or maybe just interesting. She was twenty-seven when they married — unusually late for a single Indian woman. He treated her like shit. My relatives told me he abused her badly. Anyway, when I was twelve, she had some kind of breakdown. A few months later, she killed herself. My father didn't want to be bothered with me, so I was farmed out to some of my Indian relatives who lived in Washington. I guess they got tired of me real fast because by the time I was fourteen, I was engaged, without my consent, to a thirty-five-year-old, very successful Indian businessman whose name was Singh. By the time I was sixteen, I was married. I had no say in the matter."

Stephanie winced at the thought of anyone having so little control over her own life.

Reading her reaction, Alice waved a hand as if to banish her concern. "It wasn't all that bad," she said. "Hari was very good to me. And I loved him the way a child loves a kind and gentle father. Besides, it never occurred to me that I had any options. By the time I was twenty-one, I had given birth to three sons. At twenty-two I was a widow. Hari and two of the boys, the oldest ones, were killed in an airplane crash. They were on their way to visit the kids' grandparents in New Delhi."

Alice's words hung in the air between them. Stephanie wondered if she was telling her all this to win her cooperation through sympathy. "How awful for you," she finally said.

"Yes, it certainly was then," Alice said. "It seems like such a long time ago now. Sometimes it's almost as if I dreamed it. I don't talk about it much anymore."

"Perhaps you should."

"The good part about it was that Hari left me a lot of money and a son. Mark is thirty now. The money allowed us to live comfortably while I went to college and law school. I took back my maiden name, Cutter. I'm not sure why, except I had this burning need to take back all the parts of me that had been given away to someone else." She was silent for a while.

This recounting of Alice's life had taken Stephanie by surprise. She hadn't expected anything so personal after what had transpired at the courthouse. It was becoming increasingly difficult to maintain her resentful feelings toward the woman. "Alice," Stephanie said. "What does all this have to do with Phillip King?"

"Everything. And nothing. I just want you to understand why I need you in my life."

"To help with the Enlightenment thing?" Something in Stephanie's voice could have been disappointment.

"Of course. What else?" Alice grinned a private, very devilish grin, remembering her comments to Billie about the difference in their ages. Maybe she had been wrong. Maybe Stephanie was attracted to her, after all. How flattering!

* * * * *

"Mind control with drugs," Worth French said.

"Precisely," Dexter Spencer replied.

French lit a thick cigar. The pungent smell filled the room. "Care to tell us how it's done?"

"Chemicals," Spencer said, fingering his beard.

"What kind of chemicals?"

Spencer looked him squarely in the eye. "That's the problem. I don't know for sure. That's what I need you for, French. Or more precisely, I need the facilities of your pharmaceutical company to find out what the active ingredient is."

French puffed away while he considered that fact. "There'd be a lot of uses for a chemical like that. Most of them bad, I expect."

"No different from atomic energy. It depends entirely on who gets hold of it. I'd expect the government to offer a lot of bucks for it. Hell, we can have our own government if we want to."

Munsington cleared his throat to remind them he was still in the room. He began to pontificate. "My advice would be —"

"I didn't bring you here for advice, Odell. Keep your shirt on. I'll get to you later. You interested, Worth?"

"Depends on how much money you want."

"No money. Or at least, not much. I want your facilities and the legitimacy of the Atlas Chemical name. Otherwise, what's to keep the Washington big guns from just bopping me on the head, taking the stuff and dropping me overboard somewhere? It would be a lot harder to get rid of a big company like ACI."

French sat up straighter and slid forward to lean his arms on the table. "Where is this *stuff*, Dexter, and how did you administer it to these people? So far I only have your word that this chemical exists."

"It's in the lake in small quantities, and the lake is fed by an underground spring. Maybe more than one. I found out about this substance quite by accident. You see, I noticed that people were abnormally compliant and eager to please after they had been swimming in the lake. I've had a crew digging for weeks, but so far we haven't hit the mother lode of whatever it is. I've extracted some from the lake water by simple evaporation."

"And you gave it to those people —"

"In the drinking water this evening at dinner. The bad news about the damned stuff is that it's effective for only about an hour or so. But it works very well for that period of time, as you've seen."

"There are ways around that. Might be able to develop some sort of timed release capsule or maybe a skin patch," French said thoughtfully. "What we need is enough of it to do a decent chemical analysis, then we can synthesize it. Make it synthetically."

"This is all very interesting," Munsington said, "but what's to keep people from telling the police what you've done to them?" He himself had barely avoided being convicted of fraud for misrepresenting the use of the funds for his electronic church.

"The good news is that people develop amnesia for whatever they've done under its influence," Spencer said. "Those fine people won't remember tossing their kids in the lake."

"And you put it in their drinking water?" Munsington eyed the water pitcher suspiciously and screwed up his face.

Spencer laughed loudly when he saw his expression. "The ones who've chosen to give up all their worldly materials and live here get it nearly all the time. But I won't need to drug you to get your cooperation, Odell. I'm going to do something that's right up your alley. I'm going to make you the grand prophet of this whole place. I want the public to believe that you're the power behind the throne —

the one who can make the people do whatever you tell them. The greatest spiritual leader of the century. And you're gonna eat it up."

* * * * *

Alice Cutter sat cross-legged on the floor. She had excused herself briefly to change into a pair of faded jeans and a sweatshirt. She looked as comfortable in this attire as she had in her courtroom robes. Stephanie was watching her intently, still not sure what to make of the woman.

"So you see how I feel," Alice said. "When I realized that Mark and his wife, Ruth, had fallen completely under Dexter Spencer's spell and could not be talked out of this craziness, I called the FBI. Mark is far too sensible a person to get caught up in some cult anyway, but when I found out that he had deeded over his house and his importing business to the man, I just knew something was really out of kilter. He and Ruth, as well as my year-old granddaughter, are living at the commune."

Stephanie had removed her shoes and was curled up comfortably on the sofa with her feet tucked up under her skirt. "You seem very frightened about their safety," she said.

"Well," Alice said. "I'm trying hard not to be frightened, but I am worried. And I won't stop worrying unless the FBI tells me I have nothing to worry about."

"Even so, Alice, why would the FBI take your word that something's amiss? Why wouldn't they just assume Mark liked living in a commune?"

Alice chewed on her lower lip a moment. "Let's just say I've got a friend or two in the agency. I've done a couple of favors for them in the past."

Stephanie studied the woman's face, not sure what to make of her anxiety over her son. Alice Cutter was a very complex woman, and, undoubtedly, extremely competent and totally sane. But could she simply be overreacting to the apparent loss of what was left of her family? Stephanie knew from her own work with families that no parent ever wants to face up to the idea that sometimes children take a completely different path in life from his or her own.

"And just what is it that you think I can do to help you?" Stephanie asked her.

"At the very least, Stephanie, I believe that Spencer is using some sort of brainwashing technique."

"Brainwashing? Oh, Alice! Surely you jest!"

Alice stood up and began to pace. "Just hear me out," she said. "You heard King say that several prominent citizens of Richmond have joined this commune. These aren't your young misfits who get involved with groups like the Moonies. They're fully grown, responsible, resourceful people."

"That still doesn't tell me what you want with me," Stephanie said.

"Your training as a psychologist will, I hope, allow you to make an assessment of what Spencer is doing to people. And, since you grew up in a commune, you'd know whether this place is — well — like your normal commune."

Stephanie bridled with resentment, but she chose, for the moment, to ignore the reference to the commune. "Alice, pardon me for speaking so bluntly," she said. "But it's really stupid to think that I would know anything the FBI doesn't know about. Those people are experts in all the techniques used in behavioral control. They've funded a lot of research on behavior modification and hypnosis. Cognitive restructuring is the latest thing they've sunk money into."

"Each of which has limited application," Alice argued. "I've been doing a lot of reading on the subject, but correct me if I'm wrong. Those kinds of methods require at least some degree of cooperation on the part of the person who's being influenced, don't they. A person *can* resist, can't they?"

"True. Most people can. Provided they believe what they're being asked to do is unreasonable. But the kind of influence Spencer may be using, however poorly understood it may be, is not unheard of. There seem to be ways to persuade people to cooperate with things that are totally outlandish. What about the control that Jim Jones had? His followers were adults. They left everything they owned and moved halfway around the world with him. Then apparently killed themselves and their children just because he told them to. The FBI investigated thoroughly."

"But I don't think the FBI or anybody else knows how he did it."

Stephanie shrugged, then conceded. "Probably not for sure. Some sort of depersonalization paradigm, is my guess. Like the Koreans and Vietnamese used on POWs. First they bring a person down to the lowest level of humanity so that there's no sense of self left. The Asians used starvation and punishment.

Isolation. Some say Jim Jones humiliated people publicly to accomplish the same thing. Afterward, it's a little like filling the shell that's left with whatever you want. Of course, it's not the kind of thing that we allow researchers to experiment with in this country, so we don't know much about it except what we've heard from the few soldiers who survived to return home."

"But," Alice persisted, "the unanswered question is why Jones' followers put up with it. They weren't in prison; they could have walked away at any time. No, Stephanie, I have a hunch Spencer is using something else. King and his sidekicks agree. They think maybe he's discovered some kind of new drug. But it's just a guess until we look the place over closely."

Stephanie nodded soberly. "And that's the reason for the chemist?"

"That's right. He's got to figure out some way to get blood or urine samples."

"What about the geologist? What's his part?"

"You've got me there. King pulled him in without saying anything to me. Maybe he thinks there's some kind of mineral or something right there on the grounds."

The whole idea that Alice was proposing seemed strange to Stephanie — and dangerous — if things were as she feared. What right did this woman, this stranger, have to ask her to take part in such a thing? "And you? What's your job? Or are you just going to send the rest of us out to play Russian Roulette with a madman? *If*, that is, Spencer is what you say he is." She was conscious of a dull resentment in her gut that threatened to once again overshadow the admiration she felt for Alice.

"Aside from my personal interest, I'm going along to see if Spencer's breaking any laws that would let us shut him down. But frankly, I don't have much hope for that. He's a smart cookie." She paused. "Won't you help me, Stephanie?"

Their eyes met. Alice's eyes were compelling, almost pleading.

Embarrassed, Stephanie looked away after a few seconds.

"I need you, Stephanie," Alice said softly. "You with your background and clear mind. You can see things objectively. Won't you help me? Please."

Stephanie felt sympathy and resentment together. She rubbed at her temples and closed her eyes as she spoke. "Alice, you have the wrong idea about me. I'm just like Tolkien's Hobbits. I don't like adventure. God, I need safety like a duck needs water! I managed to ruin the best relationship anyone could ever hope for because of my overblown fears. Just because I'm a psychologist, I'm not this totally well-adjusted person who can leap buildings in a single bound. I do okay helping other people in therapy, but sometimes I don't do so well when it comes to helping myself."

Alice spoke quickly. "I know all about you and Robin, Stephanie. The FBI has done a thorough investigation of your background."

Stephanie shook her head in dismay. Her face turned as white as paper. She was trying to express the indignation that had frozen her vocal cords when a knock at the front door stopped her.

Alice moved toward the foyer. "I've invited someone I think you'll want to meet," she said.

She returned with a woman of medium height and just slightly overweight. Her dark, shoulder-length hair, streaked lightly with silver, set off her gray eyes. She smiled as Alice said, "Stephanie, I want you to meet someone dear to me. This is Billie Robinson. She worked for your Aunt Mary before Mary was killed. Billie's with the FBI. She's working temporarily for the Arm. She'll be your — our — contact if you should decide to help us find out what's going on at Enlightenment."

Stephanie sat as still as stone. The name Billie Robinson was not unknown to her.

Then Alice added, "She was your Aunt Mary's lover when Mary was alive. And now she's mine."

* * * * *

"It was so eerie, Alice, to see Stephanie. She's the spitting image of Mary. A younger Mary than I ever knew, of course," Billie said, as they lay naked and side by side in each other's arms in the moonlight. "I hope you don't mind. I brought a picture of her." Billie leaned over and turned on the bedside lamp, then rummaged through her handbag on the floor by the bed.

In the dim light, Alice studied the face in the photo. "Stephanie does look a lot like her. She was beautiful. You still miss her, don't you?"

"I guess I always will. I thought I wouldn't be able to stand it when she was killed. But I do feel like some of the old ghosts have been put to rest knowing that Marvin Brennerman is safely locked

away for his part in that case we called the
Chesapeake Project. He confessed to Mary's murder
and several others once we had the goods on him."

Alice rested her head on Billie's broad shoulder.
Slowly and gently, she caressed her bare arm as she
nibbled at the soft flesh of her neck. She loved the
way her skin felt. So soft, yet firm and comfortable
to lie against. "I hope you know I don't feel at all
threatened by her memory. I'm just glad you were
able to have such a love."

"Thank you for that," Billie said. "It's important
to me that you understand."

Alice said tenderly, "How could I deny you the
memory of someone who made you so happy? If I
feel anything negative about you and Mary, it's envy.
Not jealousy. I spent so many years without really
knowing what love was. This kind of deep love that
we have, anyway. I just wish we could be together
more often, you and I. I love you so much."

Billie inhaled the clean smell of Alice's hair. She
was never quite sure how to respond when the
conversation turned to their frequent separations.
Neither of them liked being apart so much, yet
neither was willing to leave her life's work either.
Each of them acknowledged that it had taken too
many years to get where they were.

"Long-distance love affairs like ours have their
disadvantages," Billie said, and sighed deeply. "But
we know there's a good part too. Like . . . how *very*
good we are for each other when we *are* together."

With characteristic bluntness, Alice replied,
"Maybe you'd like to show me just how good that
is."

Billie reached to switch off the light, thought

better of it, and rolled back over to stare soberly into Alice's scorching blue eyes. "I'll love you forever, my sweet and wonderful Alice Cutter. My lovely judge lady. No matter how little time we have together." Billie drew her close and covered her face and her throat and her mouth with tiny kisses.

"Billie, I . . ." Alice began, but as Billie moved boldly against her, breast to breast, passion swept through her in sudden, hot waves that silenced her.

"I never get enough of you," Billie murmured. She kissed Alice hard and deep and long — as if she could store her essence away for the times when they were apart. She slid her hands possessively, but gently, over Alice's breasts and back, then moved them to her thighs and the inner softness between. The clock in the living room chimed twelve times.

"You know what happens to me at midnight?" Alice whispered breathlessly, breaking the kiss. She grinned playfully and kissed the tip of Billie's nose.

"You turn into a pumpkin," Billie said, her voice thick with desire. She turned on her side and drew an imaginary line with her finger down the damp cleft between Alice's breasts. Then she licked it as if it were covered with something sticky and sweet.

"No, darling," Alice said. "I turn into a sex maniac. But tonight I want my sex real slow and easy. You know, like drinking fine wine. Not like gulping a 7-UP!"

Billie laughed and kissed her lips with a smack. "I can't help it if I'm horny."

"You know something?" Alice asked. She let her fingers trail lightly over the curve of her lover's belly. "Tonight you're going to enjoy yourself more than you ever have — with me or anybody else."

Alice's hand moved in lazy circles over Billie's stiffening nipples, first one, then the other, as she sucked hungrily at her ear lobe.

"Sex, you mean? Or this conversation you won't stop!" Billie said, teasing.

"Sex, my love. Long, lusty, and lovely sex. Where your body and mine do unbelievable things to each other. You know what I mean? Where it's so damned good it makes your head spin!"

Her fingers moved as if on tiny spider feet to the wetness of Billie's inner thighs. She stroked the well-muscled fullness of her strong legs with fingers that were wet and slippery, relishing the familiar feel.

"Incredible! Unbelievable!" Billie managed to say as Alice slid into her with one fluid push and began the lazy thrusting, in and out, round and round, filling her, and thrilling her so that she could barely breathe.

"Believe it," Alice murmured. "And there's more."

"God! Who would have thought it?" Billie whispered. Then matching Alice's playful mood, she added, "And you such a dignified lady too. How wonderful you are, Judge Cutter! But where did you learn such wicked, wicked ways?"

Alice said nothing, but deftly leaned forward so that the tips of her breasts brushed back and forth across Billie's face and mouth.

With a moan, Billie kissed the soft dark circles and licked the stiffened nipples before she clutched Alice to her, sucking lightly, but rhythmically until she felt Alice thrust herself against her thigh. Billie's body surged with passion, but she fought against her climax.

Gracefully, Billie moved her hand downward until she felt Alice open her legs and lift her body slightly to accommodate and receive her. Alice's heat seemed to burn her as she felt a flood at her touch.

"Oh yes! I want that," Alice said. "I want to feel — pure lust!"

Billie watched her movements, fascinated.

The expression on Alice's face resembled pain more than passion, and if she had not smiled at just that moment, Billie would have withdrawn for fear she was hurting her. Billie watched transfixed as Alice arched her back and pulled her further into her. Then she was still. Dead still, as if by not moving she could hold the near-excruciating pleasure at its pinnacle.

"Incredible!" Billie said again.

Her voice seemed to break some kind of spell, for Alice began to move against her with slow, easy strokes that pulled Billie quickly along until she was matching every increasingly frenzied thrust. Billie gasped loudly, overcome by the power of their mutual passion. Then, as she heard Alice's breathing become more and more ragged, she allowed herself to move into her own climax.

They held each other close as they moved harder and faster until, at last, the tension they had aroused erupted gloriously, filling them with a blinding sensation of orgasm and joy. They moaned together with the pleasure. Then murmured mindlessly as they caressed reflexively and without consciousness. Until finally only the reflex was left.

CHAPTER FIVE

Megan Cameron arrived early for her ten o'clock appointment with Dr. Scott. When Mrs. Bateson ushered her into Stephanie's office, she kept her eyes downcast and appeared to be intimidated by her surroundings.

The wall behind Stephanie's desk was lined with books, but the rest of the room was sparsely furnished. Two chairs sat in front of the desk. Deep carpet and heavy drapes absorbed most of the sound, assuring privacy. A window on one side of the room offered up a view of Monument Avenue and

Stonewall Jackson astride his metal horse. Megan sat down stiffly in the chair most distant from Stephanie.

"How can I help you, Megan? Robin says you've been having some kind of trouble," Stephanie said in her best professional tone. She wanted to get to the point of their meeting without small talk.

"Yes. Phone calls. Robin tells me it's just some crank," Megan said, pulling a handkerchief from her purse. Her hands trembled slightly as she looked up into Stephanie's face. "But I know better. The man has called me several times. Threatening me. I really don't want to talk about it, but Robin says I have to. And she is very persuasive. She says . . . I suppose I can talk to you."

"And when he calls, what does he say?" Stephanie asked, keeping her to the point of the meeting. She didn't want to discuss Robin's role in this.

They stared at each other across Stephanie's desk, each keenly aware that the other felt uneasy. A cacophony of muffled car horns came in through the window.

Megan finally spoke. There was a tinge of a deep-south accent that Stephanie had not noticed at first. "Why, it's always the same thing. He talks about — the rape, of course. He tells me — things. Details. Things that happened that night which only he would know."

"Has Robin spoken to him on the phone or heard him speak to you?"

"Why, no. And that's the other thing. He only calls when I'm alone. I don't know how he knows. Well, actually he did call once when she was there, but when she answered, the line went dead. Dr. Scott. Stephanie. May I call you that? I'm just beside myself. I'm scared to death. I'm afraid that man will attack me again. I just don't know what I'm going to do when Robin goes back to work." She dabbed at her eyes with the handkerchief.

Seeing Megan Cameron in the neutral space of her office was not as bad as Stephanie had feared. When she shifted into her therapist mode, she could almost forget how much she resented this woman and her relationship with Robin. She looked her over with a diagnostic eye. If her face had not been so drawn, she would have been pretty. As it was, she was striking. She had the ultra-thin body of a model. Blonde hair and hazel eyes. Fashionably dressed. She looks a lot like me, Stephanie reflected. Or like I used to look. She made a mental note to begin taking better care of herself.

"Tell me a little about the symptoms you've been experiencing."

"Well, I can't eat. Can't sleep without pills. And I've begun to have dizzy spells. Last night I got up during the night and I passed out on the bathroom floor."

"And your physician found nothing wrong physically?"

Megan shook her head and drew in a deep breath. The southern accent became more pronounced. "No. Nothing. I told Robin I was all right, but she insisted that I have a checkup. Robin is so — well — you know how she is, I suppose. She's a really good person. So caring. So loving."

Stephanie was stung by the innocent comments about Robin, as if they were barbed and aimed at her. "Megan, Robin said that you insisted on seeing me instead of someone else. I really am not convinced that it's a good idea. There are a lot of good therapists in Richmond you could have gone to who could help you get through this. I expect you do need some support, but why me?"

Megan hesitated dramatically. "To tell you the truth, Dr. Scott. Stephanie. I don't put much stock in shrinks. Therapists, I should say. And I certainly wouldn't want to tell intimate . . . things to a stranger. Oh, I know we've never met," she went on quickly, "but because of Robin, well, I feel a little like I know you. And besides, I really don't think there's anything wrong with my," she hesitated again, "mental health. Do you?"

"Probably not. It would seem a natural response to feel afraid of a man who had raped you. Certainly, there's nothing pathological in that. If you do choose to see a counselor or therapist, it would only be to have someone to confide in. To talk about your fears. It's possible that you've never fully resolved your feelings about the rape, but perhaps Robin can help you with that. I understand you hadn't told her about it until the phone calls started."

"Yes. I mean, no. Perhaps I should have, but it didn't seem important to our relationship. And she has enough to worry about on her job. She takes her police work very seriously, you know."

"I know."

"She works much too hard. Too many long hours. I'm always telling her she should take it easier. Take more time off. It's not as if we need the money. I inherited quite a bit of money from my father, you know. She needn't work at all really. Robin pays little enough attention to me when she *isn't* working." There was a pout on her lips and she was picking at some non-existent lint on her blue cotton skirt.

Stephanie shifted uneasily in her chair as Megan went on. "And this shooting. Her leg, you know. I've been just heartsick and numb since that happened to her. Now these phone calls. Perhaps you could talk to her. Convince her she should stay at home. Quit that awful police force. Maybe she'll listen to you."

The impact of what the woman was saying, the irony of it, slammed straight into Stephanie's stomach. "If the two of you are having problems, Megan, perhaps you should see a couples therapist."

Megan looked up from her lint picking. There was a barely hidden challenge in her eyes; her mouth was a thin straight line drawn down at the corners. "I didn't say we are having any problems. Whatever are you trying to imply?"

The conversation was taking an unsettling turn, going straight toward an open confrontation. That was the last thing Stephanie wanted to happen. She scribbled a name and address on a piece of paper, then stood up. "I'm going to refer you to a colleague of mine who specializes in counseling rape victims. Perhaps she can find room for you in one of the group sessions. It certainly can do you no harm, and if you find you don't need it, then you can drop out if you wish."

Megan eyed her suspiciously, then nodded. "Well, it's good to know you don't think there's anything wrong with me. Thank you, Doctor." She smiled weakly and picked herself up. "Perhaps you would be so kind as to inform Robin that I am just fine."

"I think it would be better if you told her yourself."

As she watched Megan Cameron leave with her chin thrust out, she couldn't help wondering what her visit had really been about. It certainly didn't seem to be about therapy. And not about her fear of being raped again either. Was this some sort of game she was playing? Probably only time would tell.

* * * * *

It was a quarter past eleven. Stephanie buzzed Mrs. Bateson. "Has Alan Rosanowitz canceled?"

"He just this minute called. He just can't make himself leave the house today. He'll try to see you next week. Poor man. It frightens him so to have to come here."

"Agoraphobics," Stephanie muttered under her breath. They broke more appointments than they kept, but their anxiety about being in public had to be overcome somehow. Occasionally the therapy appointment gave them a reason for fighting their exaggerated fears of being with people.

"A package just arrived for you, Dr. Scott," the intercom crackled again. "The UPS man dropped it off. Shall I bring it in?"

"Yes, please."

Mrs. Bateson was a small, bird-like woman with a tendency to talk too much, too long. She claimed with pride that she was sometimes mistaken for the late actress Ruth Gordon. But it was her energy that kept Stephanie's office running smoothly.

The box was about twelve inches long, six inches wide and two inches deep. The sticker in the upper left corner read Webster Research Group. Mrs. Bateson placed it carefully on the desk.

"Don't forget you have a luncheon appointment with Billie Robinson," she said as she pulled the door closed behind her.

Stephanie nodded and picked up the strange box. She couldn't remember ordering anything from any research outfit. The taped edges slit easily and the box popped open. Underneath the mound of styrofoam half-circles lay an enormous dildo. She lifted it cautiously, brushing away the white plastic globs that clung to it stubbornly, like leeches. It was too pink and too thick and long to resemble anything real. It was battery operated. Curiously, she flipped the switch at the base of it to *ON*. Quietly, suggestively, it began to undulate like some gigantic night crawler.

She nearly laughed, until she saw the childlike block printing along the phallus's underside. Someone had used a felt-tip pen to write: USE THIS UNTIL I GIVE YOU MY REAL ONE. BITCH. G.R.

Her heart thumped hard in her chest as she reached for the phone.

* * * * *

"I got one too! How big is yours?" Alice Cutter's laugh sounded forced and too loud across the phone line.

"It's not funny, Alice. That man is dangerous!"

"You would have thought it was funny if you'd seen that big ape of a bailiff of mine walk in here with that thing in his hand. Boy, was his face red! He checks all my office mail before it comes to me."

"More of Rooney's antics, you think?"

"I expect so. Anyway, I'm working on a restraining order that will keep him away from both of us. Of course, as I told you, he can defy it. Just watch yourself. Keep your doors locked and don't walk down any unlit streets."

"That's very comforting."

"You want me to get the police to put a watch on you? You didn't want anything to do with the police when he accosted you in the parking lot."

Stephanie thought of Robin. She was living in the same house with Megan and that hadn't stopped someone from threatening her. "I guess not. Rooney's just acting out his macho fantasies. As long as he's happy harassing us through the mail and on the phone, he's probably not going to do anything else."

"Listen, Stephanie, I forgot to ask you. Did you ever talk with Rooney's wife?"

"Last week. She said she thought she would get out of town for the rest of the summer. Take the kids to visit some relatives in Charlottesville. She knows the guy is a fruitcake."

"I hope he doesn't know where she's going."

"Probably doesn't. Otherwise I doubt he'd be hanging around here aggravating us."

"Yeah. Well, you're the expert on loonies. Do me a favor, huh? When you see Billie at lunch, tell her what's happened and ask her to call me. My son Mark telephoned this morning with the message that

I should come to the commune to visit. Dexter Spencer's behind the invitation, I'm sure."

"What did you tell him?"

"That I would come this weekend and bring a friend."

"Billie?"

"You."

"The hell you say." She slammed the phone down as hard as she could.

* * * * *

The day was bright and warm. The sky was cloudless. Odell Munsington had never felt happier. Dexter Spencer was as good as his word. He was turning the spiritual leadership of Enlightenment over to him. He had conducted two hellfire-and-damnation services on Saturday and two more on Sunday. Soon everyone on the place would be looking at him with adoring eyes. Some already were. Especially the women. It was wonderful to feel that inner glow of absolute power again.

If Dexter wanted his people to meditate and eat vegetables along with the rest, that was all right too. Munsington flattered himself that he could find some justification for anything in the scriptures, even those weird things. All he needed to do was apply his golden tongue to the message and eventually he would have them believing anything he wanted. He could have them eat nothing but sweet potatoes — or even dirt — if it suited his purposes.

More important, he would soon have all the women believing that they wanted him. Couldn't stand being without him in their beds. He patted his rotund stomach. Might have to slim down a little before that happened, but with Spencer's drug, even that wouldn't matter.

Munsington smiled as he stood near the lake, watching two of the young females who worked in the kitchen take their morning swim. It was the older of the two who had his attention. She was a round, athletic blonde with dark brown eyes, an unusual combination of features that never failed to arouse him. As she stepped from the lake and began to towel her body, he could see that the narrow top of her bathing suit barely covered her breasts. The dark brown circles of her nipples peaked up playfully at him. Her suit bottom was handkerchief sized. He felt himself stiffen. He wanted her.

Perhaps if she had swallowed enough of the water from the lake while she was swimming — but he would have to be extremely careful. Carelessness had caused him to lose his power as a televangelist and he didn't want to blow this second chance Dexter had given him.

The woman walked in his direction. She was even more beautiful than he had thought. Her hips rocked back and forth in a rhythm that took his breath away.

He really wanted her. Wanted her now, but it was too risky. Even foolish.

The wanting got the best of him. "Miss," he said, as she moved near to him.

"Yes, sir. Oh, it's you, Reverend Munsington. I heard you preach last night. Nice sermon." She shook the water from her golden tresses and started to walk away.

"Where are you going — uh — what's your name?"

"I'm Maxie. Maxine, actually. I'm going to get ready to work lunch in the dining room. We have a lot of people to feed today."

"You're beautiful, Maxie. Give me your towel."

Her eyes seamed to glaze over. With only a moment's hesitation, she handed him the terry cloth beach towel. A bewildered look crossed her face.

"Maxie, will you walk over there to those bushes with me?"

"If that's what you wish," she said, and altered her course to accommodate his request. Her voice sounded normal, with no trace of any drug effect.

Maybe she just likes me, Munsington mused and felt himself grow even more rigid as they approached the foliage.

"Do you like to fool around with men?" he asked.

She hesitated as if she didn't understand the words.

"Sex," he said. "Do you like it?"

"Yes, I like it."

They were surrounded by head-tall bushes that smelled of pine and cedar. Morning glory vines had turned the space into a thicket. Munsington hadn't looked for a private place in advance, but if he had, he couldn't have chosen a better one.

"Stop here," he said.

She stopped obediently, obviously waiting for his next command.

81

"Unzip my pants."

She stared at him uncomprehendingly.

He circled her shoulders loosely with his arms. Quickly, he kissed her forehead, lips, and the top of each breast before he stepped back.

"You want to touch me, do you understand?" he said.

She stood quite still.

Maybe he had been wrong to try this. What if Spencer was wrong about the lake water? The sweat popped out on his upper lip and he glanced around to make sure they were still alone. If Spencer ever found out —

"You want me to do that?" she asked softly.

"Yes. Take out my — you know." He pushed her hand toward his crotch. Then impatiently, he unzipped his own pants and removed the engorged penis. "Now touch it, Maxie. Rub it. Hurry. Please hurry, before someone comes."

She made a noise, almost of pleading, but reached for him anyway, unable to help herself. Then lightly, she touched him.

The excitement was too much. He ejaculated instantly. Amazed at the rebellion of his own body, he watched himself spurt, uncontrollably and unexpectedly, onto the ground. Then it was over. Over in a second. The penis wilted and shriveled. He had wanted more. Much more.

The girl stared, confused, at the puddle at her feet.

"You, you . . ." Munsington choked. "Look what you did to me!"

"Maxie?" a distant voice called. "Maxie, where are you? Where did you go?"

82

Her girlfriend. Panic hit him hard in the chest and took his breath away.

"You will remember none of this, Maxie," he whispered as he stuffed the rebellious organ back into his pants. "Do you understand? Remember nothing."

"Nothing," she echoed. "Yes, sir."

"You heard my sermon last night. You liked it and you liked the music. That's all. You haven't seen me since, understand?"

"I understand. The sermon. Music."

"Now go on to work."

She headed away from him toward the dining hall.

* * * * *

"So you only met your aunt, Mary Scott, that one time?" Billie Robinson asked Stephanie. She pulled at the collar of her yellow blazer, then brushed her thick, graying hair out of her face. The restaurant was cool and dark, giving relief from the summer sun.

"When I was about ten. She and my father had some . . . philosophical differences, you might say. He hated her work. Said it was against everything he believed in. He called her a hawk and a warmonger. She called him a gutless wonder and a peacenik. Even a communist. And those were the nicer things they said to each other." Stephanie smiled. "I had never heard people yell and scream at each other like they did. People at Walden Two never raised their voices to anyone."

"Was it hard for you, living there at Walden

Two? Growing up so differently from the other kids your age?"

"It was okay. I was happy. You know how it is when you're a kid. You never question the life you live very much or think about whether your life is different from anyone else's. We went to school and worked on the farm like a lot of other kids do."

"But you weren't really raised by your parents, were you?" Billie tapped nervously at her water glass with a fingernail. Being with Stephanie was bringing back old memories of losing Mary that she thought she had put away forever.

"Not in the way you're talking about. When I was an infant, I was placed in the care of professional caretakers. Raising the kids was their job at the commune. We all lived in a dorm."

"Did you ever see your parents?"

"Sure!" Stephanie laughed. "Every day. It was just that I didn't learn to love them any more than I loved anyone else. They believed that strong bonding to one or two people, even if they are your parents, isn't a good thing. That it leads to the development of aggression and territorial defense. You know, fighting. At Walden Two, everything belonged to everyone. Even the kids."

"And do *you* believe that the way you were raised is the best way?" Billie searched through her pockets for a crumpled cigarette pack which she put on the table and looked at as if trying to resist its temptation.

Stephanie sighed deeply. "No. Oh, I don't know, Billie. I might if I hadn't read the results of the research they did on us. It didn't paint a glowing picture."

Billie raised her eyebrows in surprise. "Research?"

"Oh, yes," Stephanie said, toying thoughtfully with an ashtray on the table. "After the commune was . . . dissolved, they tested the whole gang of us who grew up there. Very thoroughly. Some psychologists from the University of Virginia, I think. They said we had developed into passive, ineffective people. One report even said we had low ego-strength. No guts. Sometimes, Billie, I think they were right. I seem to hate conflict more than most people do."

Billie shook a crooked cigarette from the pack, tamped it on her thumbnail and lit it. She tried to blow the smoke toward the ceiling, but the air conditioning pushed it back down around their heads. She quickly stubbed out the cigarette.

"They made quite a generalization, don't you think? You don't seem very ineffective to me. You're a very successful psychologist."

"One's profession isn't the only measure of success," Stephanie said dryly. "I am a passive, non-violent person. I'm not ashamed of it. I take pride in the fact that I don't get involved with movements or take up causes. And I'm certainly not your typical capitalist, dedicated to fanatic consumerism. My parents and the people in the commune taught me there was no excuse ever for hurting another human. Even if the hurting consisted of just using up more than your share of the earth, so that others have to do without."

"Is that why you don't want to help Alice Cutter? You're afraid that there'll be conflict? Someone will get hurt?" Billie asked gently.

Stephanie frowned. "It's not that I don't want to

help her. My profession is to help people who want to be helped. It's just that — just that I believe if we all took care of our own business and stopped trying to tell everybody else what they can and can't do, things would be a lot better. We pass more laws and we punish more people, and things just get worse and worse. People get worse and worse. We attack little countries that couldn't possibly do us any harm because we pass judgment on whatever they're doing. If all people stopped forming armies, then there would be no armies to fight. Our society has done some kind of crazy flip-flop, Billie. All we care about is what people shouldn't do. Don't eat this, don't drink that. Don't believe this and don't think that. We spend too much money on punishment and not enough on prevention."

"And you think Alice is trying to tell her son what he shouldn't do. That she's just passing judgment on him," Billie said flatly.

"Why shouldn't Mark Cutter live where he wants to and believe what he wants to? What ever happened to caring about what we *should* do? We tell people they *shouldn't* do all kinds of things that don't hurt society — then we arrest people for exercising what we claim is their God-given right to freedom. If we stopped having police forces and passing laws *against* things . . ." She stopped. Her chin trembled slightly.

"I've read B.F. Skinner," Billie said. "I know he's against punishment and force. I know he believes that praise for doing the good things and positive reinforcement for doing the just things will make the world a better place to live in. But a lot of selfishness and greed and just downright meanness exists in the world. Shall we just ignore it and hope it will go away? Is that what you think?"

Stephanie struggled to get her emotions under control. "I don't know what to think anymore. I used to believe punishment was the source of all evil. But maybe evil will exist in the world no matter what we do. Being a pacifist doesn't seem to have helped *my* world any. In fact, it's caused me a lot of personal trouble."

"With Robin, you mean?"

"You know about that, too? Is there anything the FBI doesn't have in my file?"

"Only I, and Alice, know about your troubles with Robin. I know you wanted her to leave the police force. I did the investigation on you, but I didn't put that in your file."

"Thanks a lot," Stephanie said sarcastically. "What are we here for today, Billie? So you can convince me to interfere in Mark Cutter's life? That I should help the FBI stop him from doing what he wants to do? Is that the kind of thing you want me to believe Aunt Mary would have done?"

"Stephanie, I believe someone is doing something to Mark against his will. I just don't know what," Billie said softly. "And your aunt would have wanted to stop it just like I do. I loved Mary very much. And she loved me. She was a fine woman. And a good woman, no matter what your father thought of her work for the FBI. She believed in what she did enough to die for it. And you can believe that I wouldn't do anything to hurt you. You look so much like her . . ." Her voice trailed away.

"But I'm *not* like her," Stephanie protested. "That's what I've been trying to tell you. Why does everyone persist in trying to make me into something I'm not!"

Billie Robinson reached out to touch her lightly on the arm. "Look, Stephanie, as far as I'm concerned, you can be anything you want to be. I just happen to agree with Alice that you're the best person for this job. All you have to do is go there. Once, if that's what you want. Look around. See what you see. You'll know if it's a typical commune or not. See if the people are unusual. Then report back to me. That'll be the end of it. No interference. No violence. Will you do it?"

Stephanie searched her feelings. The question hung between them, revolving like a silver mobile, until a waiter in jeans and a stained white apron appeared at the table.

"Is either of you Dr. Stephanie Scott?"

"I am."

"Well, a man just called. He described you to me and said to give you this message." He held out a piece of grease-stained paper.

"Your office?" Billie inquired.

The color drained from Stephanie's face as she read the message.

Billie took the paper from her. *Hope you liked the present. There's something in the James River you'll be interested in. You'll be the next one. G.R.*

"What does it mean, Stephanie?"

Sucking in her breath, Stephanie said, "God, I hope it doesn't mean — I'm not sure."

She stood up abruptly, then said, "Billie, Alice said to call her. I forgot to tell you. Tell her that I got another message from Rooney. And tell her I'll go with her to Enlightenment after all. I've changed my mind."

Billie watched, astonished, as Stephanie turned on her heel and walked out of the restaurant.

* * * * *

Stephanie had barely put her pocketbook down in the den when the phone rang. She glanced at her watch; it had taken her nearly an hour to make her way through the heavy Richmond traffic. She had pleaded illness with Mrs. Bateson and had her cancel all her afternoon appointments.

Before the phone reached her ear, she could hear the screaming in the background. "Stephanie, thank God you're home!"

"Robin —"

"On her way home from your office, Megan was attacked —"

Stephanie's face paled. Hadn't she had enough for today? Megan's screams seemed to echo through her head from the telephone. "Robin," she began evenly. Detached. "You're on the police force —"

"I know. I know. Detective Knight has already been over here. Meg talked fairly calmly to him but now she's hysterical."

"What happened?"

Robin's voice was calm as she told the story. After her appointment with Stephanie, Megan was upset and had decided to take a walk through Byrd Park on her way home. When she headed back for the car, a thin-faced man with a beard had jumped out of an old Ford and dragged her into it. They had driven around for three or four hours when he finally stopped for gas. Seeing her chance, Megan jumped from the car and ran. Then she'd flagged down a police car.

"Didn't anyone at the service station see who the man was? Maybe someone got the license plate number?"

"Knight's gone out there to question people now. We've had a tap on the phone here for several days and I'm going to see to it that she's put under twenty-four hour surveillance."

"So what do you want me to do?"

"Just talk to her, okay?"

"Robin," she said wearily, "we've been all through this. *I* can't be her therapist. I referred her to Gail Green. She works with rape cases. For tonight, either give her the tranquilizers or get her to a doctor who can sedate her."

There was a heavy silence.

"Yeah. You're right. I'll do that. I shouldn't have called you."

"Robin, is there anything wrong between you and Megan? Other than all this business, I mean."

Another long silence. "Why would you ask that?"

"Oh," Stephanie let out a long sigh, "I don't know. It's just that sometimes when people aren't getting along, they do strange things, they imagine —" She stopped herself.

Robin filled in the rest. "Imagine things, like people from the past are calling them and kidnapping them in cars? Not hardly, Stephanie, and I resent the implication."

"I know. I'm sure you do. I'm sorry. I shouldn't have said it."

Silence hung between them again until Robin said, "We'll talk again later, okay?" And she hung up.

CHAPTER SIX

The Saturday morning of the visit to Enlightenment came much too soon for Stephanie's liking. She pulled into Alice's driveway feeling bleary-eyed and grumpy from too little sleep. She had not rested well since the last message had come from Rooney.

Later, as Alice steered her Eldorado skillfully through the winding country roads toward the commune, Stephanie sat with her eyes closed. The slight rise and fall of her chest barely suggested that she was breathing.

Alice put a hand on her shoulder and shook her gently. "Better wake up, Stephanie. We're almost there."

"I'm not asleep. I was just thinking about Robin. About how she would love to be here in my shoes. She *thrives* on excitement. Thinks it's great adventure. While I . . . I would rather be hung up by my thumbs than do this."

Alice lit a Marlboro, inhaled deeply, then ground it out in the ashtray. "You aren't going to back out on me, are you, Stephanie?"

"No, I'll not back out. And I'll do what I promised. I'll get Spencer to show me as much of the commune grounds as he will and I'll talk to as many members as I can."

Alice smiled. "Good. Now try to relax. Be calm. Don't give us away when we get to Enlightenment."

"Tell that to my stomach," Stephanie said. "Besides, you don't seem too calm yourself."

Alice couldn't deny it. Her white knuckles on the steering wheel were a testimony to her state of mind. And she was craving nicotine.

The car sped another three miles through ever narrower roads before Alice lit another cigarette. At the top of a knoll, the road took a sharp turn to the left. Alice continued straight onto a dirt road. After a mile or so, a wide, metal farm-style gate appeared in the distance, blocking their path. The whole property to either side of it was fenced. Standing nonchalantly to one side was a man with a shotgun. His attention seemed focused on his grimy tennis shoes until the car drew closer. Then he raised the gun muzzle slightly and held up his hand, signaling the car to halt.

Alice stubbed out the cigarette and slowed the Cadillac. "Billie is a bad influence on me, smoking as much as she does," Alice said, as if she needed to explain her behavior as something other than nervousness. "I hardly smoke at all until I'm around her for a few days. Then it's Katie bar the door!" She stopped the car smartly, stuck her head out the window and yelled to the man, "I'm Alice Cutter. I'm expected."

The guard spoke briefly into his walkie-talkie, opened the gate and waved them through without fanfare.

After driving another dusty mile of road decorated on both sides with healthy, well-tended crops, they spied a long, narrow, cedar-sided building with a parking lot filled with automobiles. A sign over the door said OFFICE, but no one was in sight. Old and twisted oaks stretched out their branches in canopy fashion, making the air seem cool and damp.

"Pretty place," Stephanie commented as she got out of the car. She and Alice had worn jeans and solid walking shoes for the trip.

"At one time this property belonged to some off-beat church. Brothers and Sisters of the True Light or something like that. They used the place as a retreat. Held meetings and conferences here. There was even a claim that there were healing springs around somewhere."

Stephanie said, "Perfect location for a community like this. I guess they grow most of their food in the fields we passed coming in. People in communes usually try to be as self-sufficient as they can be."

"May be," Alice muttered, "but somebody here didn't seem to mind taking Mark's money."

As Alice reached up to knock, the door opened as if someone had been watching for them.

To Stephanie's surprise the man at the door was Roger Plank, vice-president of a local bank. He had processed the loan for her car only a few months ago.

Plank was dressed in leather-thonged shoes and a long, khaki-colored, shirt-like garment tied tight at the waist with a small rope. It struck Stephanie that his face was peaceful, nearly placid, and his manner serene. She had thought him a rather unpleasant, tense man when she had met him at the bank. In fact, he had acted decidedly irritated when she had made a minor mistake on the application form. But at the moment he seemed not to recognize her. Perhaps he had forgotten. Stephanie decided not to call attention to their previous meeting.

"Please take a seat, my friends," Plank said, moving about the room as if it were a hushed cathedral. He didn't introduce himself, and seemed comfortable to take the roll of servant rather than equal. "Mr. Spencer will be with you shortly."

The room had a simple, rustic look. It was long and narrow, covering nearly the length of the building. There were two plain pine tables and several wooden chairs. Two doorways led to more rooms in the back and side, but the doors were securely closed. In place of air conditioning, a pair of paddle fans on the ceiling stirred the warm afternoon air. And there were no pictures or decorations of any kind on the pine-paneled walls.

Plank gestured toward a table near the back of the room which was covered with glasses, cups, and serving dishes. "May I offer you some chamomile tea?" he said. "And if you are hungry, we have kohlrabi, broccoli, carrots, and cauliflower with a homemade vegetable dip. All grown right here, of course. No doubt you saw some of our gardens as you came in." His face beamed with obvious pride.

Stephanie would have asked for the tea, but before she could answer, a door opened and a voice boomed, "Well, Judge Cutter! Greetings! And welcome! What a pleasure to finally meet you!"

Alice crossed the room to meet the tall man. "Mr. Spencer? How do you do?"

Spencer's feet were sandaled and he was dressed in a brown robe with the hood laid back. He looked like a holy man. Perhaps a monk. "Yes, I'm Dexter Spencer. One hears such wonderful things about you, Judge Cutter! We think so much of Mark and Ruth here and, naturally, we are all in love with baby Alicia."

Alice shook his extended hand, then turned toward Stephanie. "This is Dr. Scott. Stephanie Scott. I invited her to accompany me when she expressed a personal interest in your . . . community. You see, Mr. Spencer, she grew up in the Walden Two commune. It's considered a pioneer in . . . such things, I've been told."

Stephanie inhaled deeply as Spencer moved in her direction, but his smile seemed genuine and she immediately decided that the man did not *look* like the monster she had expected, in spite of his rather ominous black eyes. She forced some of the stiffness out of her neck and shoulders as she returned his smile.

"Ah, yes, Dr. Scott," he said warmly, as if he had expected her. "Walden Two. A fine, fine place. Too bad it fell into financial difficulty and had to be closed. Too much drug use there, it was said, but I'm sure that was only a vicious rumor."

Stephanie blanched. "Yes, I've heard those rumors, too, Mr. Spencer. But I was young when it closed. I'm not sure what really happened."

"I have often suspected that people who object to the communal way of life start such nasty gossip," Spencer said, then looked pointedly at Alice. "No doubt in Richmond one hears outrageous things about our place here. At any rate, we hope not to have bad luck at Enlightenment. We use no drugs and we're lucky enough to be quite secure financially."

Alice bristled at the reference to money and said pointedly, "One does *hear* that you're willing to take . . . large donations, Mr. Spencer. Perhaps that accounts for your . . . *good luck*?" She shot him a look of disapproval he could hardly miss.

Spencer fingered the frizzy hair on his cheeks, aware that he had said the wrong thing to Alice. "Yes. Well. People have been generous. Praise God." Then nodding in the direction of several straight-backed uncomfortable looking chairs, he said, "Won't you sit down, please. Mark will be along."

An awkward silence hung over them until Stephanie cleared her throat and said, "Perhaps you would be willing to give me a tour of your commune while Judge Cutter visits with her family, Mr. Spencer. I must confess I sometimes miss the serenity of the commune atmosphere. And I'd love to see how your place is run."

Spencer took a fleeting moment to study Stephanie's face. Then he flicked his eyes to Alice and back to Stephanie before he finally answered, "Most certainly, lovely lady, you'll get the deluxe tour. It's so wonderful here, I love showing people around! And if you find Enlightenment to your liking, perhaps you'll come back again. You know, we have weekend workshops and seminars, as well as religious meetings. Some of our friends drop by regularly after work to meditate and recharge their batteries, as they like to say! Perhaps you'll see fit to join us."

"Perhaps I'll do that some time," Stephanie said, without conviction. At the moment she was just eager to complete the bargain she had made with Alice.

"One does not give up the ways of a commune easily," Spencer added.

Outside the window, Stephanie could see several people sitting on the grass, eyes closed, hands folded, faces bland. Others sat in groups, apparently carrying on intense discussions. Behind the people, a small lake sparkled in the sun.

"I still practice meditation of a sort," Stephanie said, thinking of the tropical fish. And she unexpectedly found herself wanting to believe that Enlightenment was on the up and up, so that she could look forward to spending time here in the future. If something *is* amiss here, she mused, you can't tell it from looking at those people.

Without warning, the front door burst open.

"Mother! I'm so happy you've come. What a surprise!" The young man was obviously Alice's offspring. He was about thirty. Thin, but muscled and wiry. Skin dark. Hair black where Alice's was graying, but it was the eyes that gave it away. They were sapphire blue.

Alice answered, "It's the only way I can see you since you won't come home any more." But she hugged her son tightly to her before she asked, "Where's my granddaughter?"

"Ruth has her in the infirmary," Mark said. "She hasn't been feeling well. But don't worry. She'll be fine. Just a little summer cold, I imagine."

Stephanie and Spencer stood up in unison. "My friend, Stephanie Scott," Alice said to Mark.

"Hello," Mark said pleasantly.

Stephanie searched his handsome countenance for clues that something might be wrong, but found nothing other than his face appeared to be a little pale and drawn.

"Let me get some keys from my office," Spencer said, "and we shall leave you alone to talk while I show Dr. Scott the grounds. Enjoy your visit."

* * * * *

When the door closed behind Dexter and Stephanie, Alice unobtrusively stuck a dime-size microphone to the bottom of the nearest chair. Billie had given her a pocketful of the tiny bugs and instructions to place them wherever she could without risking being seen. Then she turned to face Mark. "Are you and the family really all right?" she asked.

"Mother," Mark began. "You know I love to see you, but I hope you haven't come here to hassle me again about leaving the commune." His face was a mask of stubbornness. They had been over this ground before.

"You don't look well," Alice said.

"Fatigue," he said. "I've been working hard — really working physically — for the first time in my life. It's good for me. It's for everybody's good, as Spencer says. I'm fine and I'm healthy."

"What kind of work are you doing?"

"Digging. Excavating, I should call it. I'm learning to be an archaeologist. Spencer says the remains of a village dating back to colonial times are here on the property somewhere. You know, Mother, like they've found in Williamsburg."

"You don't know anything about archaeology, Mark." She took his large hand in hers. It was covered with blisters. "Besides, that man is just using you like a common laborer. Look at your hands!"

"Don't be such a snob, Mother. There's nothing wrong with *common* labor! Spencer says it's good for the soul!"

"But it's not good for the body that's not used to it. And you've never been the outdoor type. Besides, Mark, you're different since you've come here. You've changed. That man is doing something to your head."

"Different from what, Mother? Different from you? Different from your materialistic friends? Just because I'm more concerned about my own soul than I am about making money or controlling society? Spencer says . . ."

"Spencer says! Spencer says! You still don't look well," Alice persisted, shaking her head in exasperation. Then she made a face at him and said teasingly, "Besides, you can't fool mother nature."

He smiled at his mother. "Mother nature, my foot! You hate any space that isn't centrally heated or air conditioned!" Mark said. "But all right, I suppose I can't fool you. I've had something like the flu. Headaches, muscle aches, nausea. The whole nine yards. But it's all over now. Besides, you can't blame the commune for a virus."

"Sounds like what you said Alicia has."

"The commune doctor has seen her — and me. There's nothing to worry about."

"Is Ruth okay? She seems to have had . . . something else to do every time I've been here. I know she doesn't care much for me, son, but she could take the time to say hello."

"Oh Mother, please! Ruth *does* like you. It's just that Spencer says it's important for Ruth to be with Alicia just now."

"Mark, why *must* you believe everything that man says?" She put her hand on his shoulder and looked pleadingly into his eyes.

Mark stepped backward so quickly that he staggered and almost would have fallen had he not steadied himself on the back of the nearby chair. "Sorry, Mother. I'm okay."

Alice tilted her head to one side, as if trying to see inside him. She knew that further verbal probing would get her nowhere.

"Yes, son," she said. "I know you're all right. Let's just sit down and talk over whatever it was you wanted to see me about."

"I don't remember," he said, but he sat down

quickly, as she had instructed. His skin turned pasty white and a look of confusion crossed his face.

"Mark?" Alice cried, alarmed.

"It's nothing! Nothing," he said. "Just some stomach cramps left over from the flu. A little dizziness." Abruptly, he seemed okay again.

"Why did you call me, son?"

"I don't know."

"Are you frightened of Spencer?"

"No! I don't know," he said. He drew a deep breath, and a look of bewilderment shadowed his face. "I remember calling. I remember wanting to talk to you. But I can't remember . . ."

She watched him anxiously. "Mark, listen to me! You have to get away from this place!"

For a moment, he seemed to teeter on the brink, suspended on the edge of decision. Then his face cleared and he looked calm and in control again.

"Don't be ridiculous, Mom. I like it here. It's good for me to be here. And for Ruth and Alicia. In fact, it's for everybody's good. Spencer says so."

"Mark, what is going on here?" Alice said urgently. "What is Spencer doing to you? The man is a . . ."

Suddenly Mark jumped up and gazed down at her with a furious expression on his face. Alice saw that his breathing was shallow and his eyes were glazed. She reached for his hand to calm him but he jerked it back.

"Mother," he managed to say in a trembling voice. "Don't come back here. You're wrong about everything. About me. About Spencer. About Ruth and Alicia. Don't ever come back here!"

"Stop it, Mark!"

Suddenly Mark pushed past her, threw open the door and ran.

Shocked by his anger and defiance, yet frightened in her heart for him, Alice ran after him. By the time she reached the porch, he was out of sight.

As she turned back to the office building, she was overwhelmed by a feeling of helplessness. Something was terribly wrong here, but what could she do about it? What in God's name could any of them do?

*　*　*　*　*

Stephanie accompanied Dexter Spencer through the commune living quarters, which were individual cabins tucked back in the woods, and the dining hall. The buildings were all simple and spotlessly clean. All were empty. When they finally turned back in the direction of the lake, they walked slowly, enjoying the day. A well-kept, emerald-green lawn gave the area around the lake a park-like appearance.

"Do you approve of what you've seen?" Spencer asked. He went on without waiting for an answer. "I must confess I've been hoping you'd come here, Dr. Scott. I've heard about you in town. Asked around about you, in fact. You have a reputation as an excellent therapist."

Stephanie looked up at him, startled and unnerved. Even though Phillip King had said she and the others were on Spencer's list of potential commune members, she had not let herself believe it.

But why else would he have been asking about her? She opened her mouth to speak, but Spencer continued.

"Do you like Enlightenment?"

"Yes, it's beautiful," Stephanie replied. "But may I ask just *why* you were asking about me?"

Spencer laughed. "Of course that must have sounded strange. Actually, Dr. Scott, I have been thinking about hiring a psychologist as part of our staff. Encounter groups never hurt anyone. Perhaps some of our people would profit from it. Don't you agree?"

"If I could speak with some of the people here, Mr. Spencer, I might be able to give you a better answer. Pardon me for saying so," she said boldly, "but if I didn't know better, I'd think you were deliberately keeping me from speaking with anyone."

"In due time," Spencer said. "I wanted you to form your own opinion of the place first. You know, absorb the atmosphere. Get the feel of the place, as they say."

"Yes, of course," she murmured. That seemed reasonable, but at the same time she wondered if she was being too gullible.

"Perhaps there are some people up ahead you could speak with," he said, and pointed.

Fifty yards away, on the far bank of the lake, she saw another building almost obscured by a stand of thick pines which had grown over with English ivy. Had she been slightly farther away, she wouldn't have been able to see it at all. Its unkempt appearance seemed totally out of place in the manicured surroundings. Its walls were dirty and unpainted and it looked as if someone had taken pot shots at the windows with rocks.

"What's that building?" she asked.

"You'll see," Spencer said quietly.

"It looks like a church. Perhaps it's from the time the People of the Light owned the land?"

"I'm afraid I don't know when it was built. It was here when I bought the place. It's very old. And falling down." Spencer took her arm to guide her in the direction of the old church.

As they drew closer, she could see that its walls were indeed crumbling, but the building had been carefully reinforced with new timbers. Through the open door she spotted a half-dozen men in work clothes pushing wheelbarrows; some were filled with copper-colored dirt. She watched spellbound as one of the men disappeared into the ground, as if eaten up by the great gaping cavern. Then another appeared at the lip of the hole with a full cart.

From the side of the building a tall, thickly built man in shorts and a T-shirt appeared. His eyes were hard and his face grim. He held a double-barreled shotgun across his chest. "Stop right there," he said.

Shocked, Stephanie reached behind her and clutched at Spencer's robe. She felt herself trembling. Her voice was pitched high when she said, "Is he going to shoot us? Do you know him?"

"It's all right, Bob! It's me, Spencer!" Spencer yelled to the man. He placed a hand on Stephanie's shoulder and patted her gently. "There, there. You needn't be afraid. No one will hurt you, Dr. Scott. You shouldn't have so many doubts about me."

She turned to study his face for a moment, not

sure whether to believe him or not. "Then why is he here with that gun? What is this place?"

"He's a member of Enlightenment. He's just guarding the building."

"From what?"

"From — nosy people. People who don't belong. You know that communes have enemies."

Stephanie said suspiciously, "Yes, but the use of guns is unheard of in communes. What's going on here, Spencer? Are you doing something illegal?"

Spencer laughed. "Illegal? No. Just something I don't want people in town to know about. But you could learn a great deal from me, Dr. Scott."

Stephanie turned back to stare at the man whose finger was curled tightly around the trigger of the shotgun. "I know all I need to know about guns and violence," she said shakily. "You are up to something here, aren't you?"

Spencer didn't answer the question. Instead he withdrew a tiny pistol from the pocket of his robe. "Come over here, Bob."

At his command, the man turned sharply in military fashion and approached them.

"Why don't you put this pistol in your mouth, Bob, and pull the trigger," Spencer said.

Stephanie gasped. Spencer held her by the shoulder.

The man reached for the pistol, then seemed confused about what to do with the shotgun.

"Put your shotgun on the ground and take the pistol."

"Yes, sir."

"My God, Spencer!" Stephanie said. "You can't do this!"

"Bob, do what you were told to do."

Stiffening just for a moment, the man placed the gun in his mouth and pulled the trigger.

Horrified, Stephanie tensed for the explosion that followed and jammed her hands over her ears. She opened her eyes slowly. The man was still standing, intact. His expression was blank.

Spencer threw back his head and laughed. It hit Stephanie immediately that the gun Spencer had given the man wasn't loaded, but the realization did not stop her trembling. She was sure Spencer could hear her heart beating. She was as furious as she was scared.

Spencer grinned broadly as he instructed the man to go back to his post. Replacing the pistol in his robe, he said, "I hope that didn't frighten you too badly, my dear. Just a little lesson in behavioral control for you, good doctor."

"You expect me to believe he didn't know that gun wasn't loaded?" Stephanie asked indignantly.

"A simple demonstration, my dear. The people at Enlightenment do exactly as I tell them. *Exactly.* But you can believe that Bob knew the gun wasn't loaded if it pleases you. Actually I thought you might be interested in how it's done — controlling people I mean — you being a psychologist."

She clenched her teeth to keep them from chattering. She was on the edge of blind panic. But she knew that to panic would be a mistake. Possibly a fatal mistake. She had to stay calm, for if Spencer actually had the kind of control over the people at Enlightenment that he wanted her to believe he had, he was presenting her with the opportunity to find out how it was done. This was the information Alice had asked her to get.

"Of course, I'm interested," she said. "The gun — it startled me. That's all."

"Then why don't we go to the dining room and get some lemonade. It's hot out here today. Then I'll tell you whatever you want to know. I'm not trying to hide anything from you, my dear doctor."

Spencer led her back to the dining hall without speaking. The room seemed darker than it had before and strangely quiet. He motioned her toward a side door. "This is my private dining room. Please go in."

She stood uncertainly for a moment. Then pushed the door open. When she turned, Spencer stood in the doorway. The pistol was in his right hand.

"What are you going to do to me?" Stephanie gasped.

"Why nothing, my dear. Besides, you don't believe this gun is actually loaded, do you? Or have you changed your mind?"

"What do you want from me?"

"Nothing. I told you. I just want to be sure you enjoy the lemonade. And I'm going to tell you some secrets about Enlightenment. Then you'll forget we ever had this little talk. You'll see. This is for everyone's good."

* * * * *

"What did you find out?" Alice asked as soon as she and Stephanie were off the commune grounds and on their way home.

"Nearly nothing. And I think he showed me the whole place. At least he didn't *seem* to be hiding anything. There's a dilapidated chapel left over from when it was owned by that church. The other buildings are practically new. They've built their own new chapel. The dining room is nothing special. The living quarters are austere. They — the spiritual leaders — encourage asceticism, Spencer said."

"So you saw nothing unusual?"

Suddenly Stephanie felt as if she were struggling to remember something. Some troublesome, forgotten memory that kept evaporating as soon as she came near it. After some hesitation, she answered, "Pretty much like Walden Two."

"What did you think of Spencer?"

Stephanie frowned and bit her lower lip. Some wispy memory sat on the edge of her consciousness again, but she couldn't bring it to mind. And she felt a little dizzy. "I'm glad it's over," she said, rubbing her temples.

"Are you all right, Stephanie? The man didn't do anything to you, did he?" Alice touched her arm.

"No. He didn't do anything to me. He did seem to know a lot about me though. He knew about my practice. Said he had asked about me in the city. Maybe Phillip King was right about my being on his list of future recruits."

"You think this Spencer is straight up? Not some kind of con man?" Alice was preoccupied with her own problems.

"Search me. He seemed nice enough to me."

"You think he has these people taking drugs?"

"Nobody looked drugged. Just very . . . peaceful. What did you think?"

Alice thought a moment before she answered. "Mark's been having some kind of blackout spells. He didn't remember he had invited me to visit."

"He looked tense to me," Stephanie said.

"Said he'd had the flu," Alice replied.

Stephanie answered, "Well, then that could account for the blackouts. Especially if he ran a high fever."

"Yeah," Alice said, sounding unconvinced. "I suppose. But look at this." She held out a small note pad.

"What's so strange about that?"

"The Atlas Chemical International logo. I picked it up off the table at Enlightenment. I can't help believing that Spencer is drugging people to get them to do what he wants."

"Maybe one of the commune members works at ACI and just left it there or something."

Alice sighed. "Yeah. You're probably right. I'm ready to grasp at straws, I guess. Maybe I just can't face up to the fact that Mark has left — and taken his family away from me. Maybe he has a right to blow up when I interfere."

Stephanie said, "You know, Alice, I wouldn't worry. In fact, I think I might just go back out to Enlightenment myself. Not to live. Just to visit. Group meditation never hurt anybody."

* * * * *

Billie Robinson sat on Alice's den sofa with her feet curled up under her, the phone between her shoulder and chin as she took notes on a yellow legal pad. A cigarette dangled from her lips, the smoke circling upward, causing her to squint as she spoke with Phillip King. "Faint traces of lithium salts in the urine and that was all he could identify? No drugs?"

She listened. "I guess that would have been too easy. How did your chemist get the urine samples?"

Billie hooted, then broke into a coughing fit. When she was calm again, she said hoarsely, "Somehow I just can't see Jason Jefferies volunteering for latrine duty, much less stopping up the toilets and dipping out little bottles full of pee! But I must admit that it was clever. What about MacIntosh?"

She absorbed the information. "We were lucky the university had the facilities to do the chemical analysis so quickly, but they aren't really equipped for the geological stuff. How long will it take for the FBI lab to analyze the ore samples?"

She absent-mindedly shuffled through some papers on the sofa as King promised to have it done as soon as humanly possible. "If that shows nothing," she told him, "I'm going in there and take a look for myself, but I'll put that off until we've heard from the geology analysis. Listen, Phil, I want you to check something out for me. A group of religious fanatics used to own the place. Let's see," she said, looking at the scrap of paper in her hand. "They called themselves something like Brothers and Sisters of the True Light. Find out what happened to them and get back to me, okay?"

She leaned back and ran her fingers through her silver-streaked hair. For a while she just sat on the sofa, staring out the window and thinking about people who make deals with God. And others who seem to align themselves with the Devil.

CHAPTER SEVEN

Stephanie pulled into her own driveway about four that afternoon, relieved that the trip to Enlightenment was over. But she was not relieved to see the bright blue BMW parked in the driveway. She knew it from somewhere, but it wasn't until she saw the disheveled figure sitting on the doorstep that she remembered. Andrew Brown had been driving it the day he had come to her house to persuade her to do the psychologicals on his client, Greg Rooney.

Brown wore a wrinkled short-sleeved shirt of

white oxford cloth, a green and yellow tie, and black slacks. His dark hair needed cutting and there was a blue-black stubble on his cheeks. He stood up wearily as she approached and slung his suit jacket over his shoulder. He ambled toward her.

"I know I look like shit," he said without preamble. "I got a call from the police early this morning. How they found me, I'll never know. I was at . . . a friend's house. Spent the night. Anyway, they wanted me at the police station right then, so I haven't been home yet." He scratched at his beard as Stephanie opened the house and led him inside.

"Something tells me your being here can mean nothing but bad news, Brown. Tell me I'm wrong," Stephanie said.

He talked rapidly as he followed her into the den. "I just wanted you to know they found Greg Rooney's wife in the James River yesterday evening. Shot in the back of the head."

"I'll put on some coffee," Stephanie said automatically and headed for the kitchen. Her stomach turned tiny flips as she thought of Rooney's note. Would she be the next one he went after? She needed time to digest Brown's information without his presence.

When she returned, she offered him a shot of whiskey for his coffee, then dumped some of the brown liquid into her own cup. "What about the children?" she asked him.

"The police don't know where they are," he said. "They've disappeared from the relative's home. The detective in charge of the case seems to think Rooney might have them. But it's possible they got scared and ran. God knows what all they've seen in their young lives."

"Why'd the police want to talk to you?"

"Rooney threatened to kill me when I lost his case. I told the cops, but he never did anything. Now I'm not so sure he won't try to get me."

Fear flitted across Stephanie's face. She took a healthy swallow from the coffee cup to steady herself. "He's threatened me too. And Judge Cutter."

"They told me at headquarters. I expect they've been trying to get hold of you, but I just wanted to tell you myself." He looked down at his feet for a moment. "I feel sort of responsible, getting you involved in this case and all. And I wanted to tell you something else. I'm ashamed to spring this on you now, after all that's happened, but you should know that Rooney served six years in prison some time back for attempted murder. He tried to kill his girlfriend with a gun."

"Damn!" Stephanie said. "And Elizabeth married him anyway?"

"It was a long time before he met her. She didn't know anything about it."

"But *you* did! And didn't mention it to me? Of all the —! You slimeball!"

Brown emptied his cup in one gulp and rose to leave. "I guess I deserve that. All I can say in my own defense is I was hired to do a job, too. Just like you. I didn't have a chance in hell of winning his case if everybody knew about his record. I figured his wife would hire a lawyer who'd present that evidence. Shocked the shit out of me when she didn't, but it wasn't up to me."

115

"She didn't have the money, you idiot!"

"Still —" Brown set the cup down and hitched up his pants. "I just do the best I can at making my own way in the world. My clients are a little like yours — not always the image of mental health — but, somebody's got to help 'em. Right, Dr. Scott?"

"Thanks for the philosophy, *mister* Brown," she said.

"Think what you have to about me," he said. "But don't say I didn't warn you."

He turned as he went out the door, digging through his pants pockets for his keys. "Do be careful, you hear?"

* * * * *

Stephanie tried to pull her thoughts together. She had not believed that she was in any real danger as long as Rooney was playing games with her and Alice, but with Elizabeth Rooney dead, what did he have to lose? Another murder or two on his hands wouldn't make much difference. With his record, they'd put him in the darkest hole they could find and cement the opening. She was about to start on her second cup of coffee when someone knocked at the door. She eased the door open without removing the chain and was startled to find Robin standing there.

"May I come in? I won't stay long. I was in the station when Andrew Brown came in. Detective Knight, Les Knight, told me about . . . the things Greg Rooney's done to threaten you. The phone calls and the dildo. Why didn't you tell me?"

Stephanie sighed a tired sigh. She had had

enough for one day, but she pushed open the screened door and stepped aside. "Come on in. I'll get you some coffee."

Robin followed her to the kitchen, but stood stiff and uneasy. "Why didn't you tell me?" she asked again.

"There was nothing to tell, Robin. He hadn't done anything he could be arrested for."

"What about assaulting you in the parking lot of the courthouse? What do you call that? Why in God's name didn't you report that to the police?"

Stephanie looked at her curiously. "How did you know about that?"

"I got a copy of the injunction Judge Cutter filed. It was all in there. I told Les I would find you and tell you about the murder, but Brown wanted to do it."

"Rooney didn't actually assault me. Nothing that would hold up in court anyway. They might have gotten him for drunk and disorderly, but he'd have been out on bail and mad as a hornet in a few hours. And he might have really hurt me then. I decided not to risk it. Besides, you might even say I assaulted him back — with my car keys. And as for the other thing, there's no proof he sent it and I would have felt like an idiot asking the police to fingerprint a dildo!"

"If I had known, I'd have found that little asshole and reamed him a new one. I know how to put the fear of God into the likes of him!" Robin's face had twisted into a mask of ferocity.

"I know you do, Robin, but you know how I feel about that sort of thing."

Stephanie put a hand to her forehead. A wave of

dizziness swept through her. The emotional impact of events of the day had been great. So great that a physical reaction could not help but follow. And she hated it when Robin took this kind of macho stance.

"Violence breeds violence and all that," Robin responded. "I know what you think. But you should have called me."

"It seems to me," Stephanie said, her voice not without sarcasm, "you've got enough on your mind right now. And speaking of Megan, how is she?"

Robin hesitated briefly. "Well, since we put the tap on the phone the rapist hasn't called. But now he's started sending her written threats. Look at this. Not much of a poet, is he?"

She pulled a tattered sheet of paper from her pocket. The letters of the message were cut out of newspapers and magazines and pasted on the page. Melodramatic, like something out of a low-budget movie.

> *Blue-eyed bitch, raped in a ditch*
> *I road her around in my car*
> *She thinks I'm a flop*
> *Cause her girlfriend's a cop*
> *But she won't get very far.*
> *I'll get you yet, whore.*

"My God! How awful." Stephanie shuddered, remembering Rooney's threatening note. If Robin hadn't been there, she would have buried her head in her hands and cried uncontrollably.

"This is the third one. No fingerprints. No postmark. They just appear in the mailbox in a plain envelope. The cheap kind you can buy at any discount store in town."

"My God! My God!" Stephanie exploded in spite of herself. "When is it all going to end? All this violence against women! A woman really does need a man, doesn't she? To protect her from other men! That's what being a heterosexual woman is all about, isn't it? It isn't about love. It isn't about caring. It's a protection racket. Sometimes I think, Robin, that men are a separate species or maybe from another planet. Do you have any idea how many battered wives I see in a week? Do you have any idea how many fathers rape their baby daughters? The government claims to have a war on drugs. How about a war on men? How about taking them all and . . ."

She stopped herself, surprised at the emotion that had erupted in her gut. Tears welled up in her eyes and trickled down her cheeks.

Robin stepped forward to encircle her within her arms. Suddenly Robin was holding Stephanie, her face in her hair. Then they were kissing, first gently, then fiercely, with passion.

"Stephanie, Stephanie," Robin said. "You smell so good. Like you."

"Oh God, Robin. I've missed you so much. I've never stopped loving you. I *need* you."

They were naked in a moment's time. Robin began kissing Stephanie's breasts, caressing them greedily with her mouth until they were wet and slick with her saliva.

Stephanie's lips were at Robin's ear, licking the rim, then sucking her earlobe. She held her body to her, her hands on her hard buttocks as she flicked her tongue suggestively in and out of the tiny ear opening.

Robin rubbed her hands gently across Stephanie's crotch until she felt the wetness soak her fingers. One hand found her buttocks and she used the slickness to part the slender cheeks and gently caress the edge of the sensitive opening there.

The electrifying pleasure made them weak, so that they could no longer stand.

As they slid to the kitchen floor, Stephanie murmured, "Love me like you used to. Don't hurry."

But they thrust their bodies tight together and began the rocking. Stephanie squeezed Robin's buttocks, hard as stone, and pulled her closer to her, matching every mind-numbing stroke, until they both peaked quickly, climaxed together, then coasted slowly down as each held tight to the other. Murmuring softly, incoherently, and holding on with desperation.

When the heat had completely died, Robin disengaged herself and rolled over on her back. The kitchen floor smelled of lemon wax.

The sound of the real world — distant traffic, car horns and sirens, children crying and mothers calling — pushed its way into their ears, bringing them back to reality. Bringing them abruptly back from the mountain of their mutual pleasure.

"What have we done, Steph? What the hell have *I* done? I — I have a commitment to Megan." Robin covered her face with her hands.

Stephanie's nostrils filled with the musky odor of her own lubrication as Robin's hands moved past her head. At another time she would have thought that sexy, but now it aroused no feeling other than emptiness. Robin's words jolted her as if she had struck her in the face.

As quickly as she could, Stephanie rose from the floor and picked up her shirt. She stepped into her jeans and zipped them loudly. "I suppose you're going to try to tell me that this was all just physical."

"Don't be upset. I — Megan —" Robin looked genuinely bewildered.

"Do you allow yourself to have these little *flings* often, Robin? Did you do that when you lived with me or is this something you've just started since you moved in with Megan?" Stephanie buttoned her shirt and stuffed it roughly into her pants. Then she gathered up Robin's clothes and tossed them toward her.

Reluctantly, Robin took them and began to dress. "I was always faithful to you. I never should have left you, Steph. I don't know what else to say."

Stephanie's eyes were as flat and cold as her voice. "Well, I know what to say. Get the hell out of my house and out of my life and don't come back. I never, you heard me — never — want to see you again."

It was much later when the tears came. After Robin and the anger had gone, the sadness and grief flooded in to fill the space.

CHAPTER EIGHT

More than two weeks went by before Dexter Spencer got the news from Worthington French about the analysis of the ore samples. Billie Robinson heard from Phillip King that same day, about three in the afternoon when she was alone at Alice's.

"It's mostly lithium chloride or something chemically similar to it. The same thing we found in the urine samples. But there's something else in these rocks, Billie. Traces of an element known to the agency as lodestar."

"Never heard of it," Billie said.

"Neither have most chemists. You won't find it on your standard element chart. We *have* uncovered some records of medieval alchemists that refer to something like it. This is just a guess, mind you, but we don't think there's much of it on our planet. It may be something that came into the earth's atmosphere as part of a meteorite. Or on an alien space ship, if you believe in such things. So when it's been found, it's in a very localized area."

"Space ship, huh? Like kryptonite in the old Superman comics? Does it turn people into hundred-pound weaklings, or what?" Billie laughed her deep laugh.

"Don't be funny, Billie. Lodestar isn't funny stuff. In fact, it makes people so fuckin' suggestible they'll do anything they're told to do, no matter how crazy or awful. It's the most powerful method of mind control known to the agency."

"You're making this up, King. Don't shit me now."

"Not on your life. I swear to God it's the truth. This information about lodestar is strictly classified, Billie. Your ears only."

Billie gripped the phone so hard her knuckles turned white. Then she erupted, "I don't believe this! If you're telling the truth, Phil, the United States has the most powerful tool on earth. Why all we'd have to do is —"

"Slip Saddam Hussein a lodestar mickey and make him follow orders like a good little puppet, right? Wrong. Lodestar has its problems. The stuff is only effective for fairly short periods of time, for one thing, so you'd have to keep giving a steady dose of

123

it in order to have any control beyond . . . oh, about an hour or two. And it's as toxic as hell. It takes awhile to kill because it has to have time to build up in the liver and turn it to stone. But it'll do it eventually if it's given repeatedly. Anyway, looks like your Enlightenment place is loaded with the stuff."

Billie shook her head in dismay. Suddenly her skin felt cold and clammy. Danger was no stranger to her, but this was something else. "Jesus Christ and Mother Mary!" she exclaimed. "Imagine what could happen if this stuff got into the wrong hands. What if a Khomeini or a Castro were to get hold of it?"

"What if your garden-variety, man-on-the-street, power monger got hold of it? With lodestar, it wouldn't take a world leader to wreak havoc, once he — or she — realized what it will do to people. My best guess is that your friend Spencer knows. Probably he's just experimenting now, trying to figure out just what he *can* do with it. You have to stop him, Billie."

"But how, Phil? I mean, think about it. Spencer owns the land and just because it has this lodestar on it doesn't make his commune illegal. We still have to catch him doing something wrong, if he is."

"You're having doubts about that? I thought you were convinced your friend's family —"

"Yeah. Yeah. I was convinced. I am still. But we've had the main building bugged for a couple weeks, recording everything, and so far *nada*."

"Two weeks isn't very long, Billie."

"Certainly you're right, but if the people at

Enlightenment *are* being given lodestar, we've got to stop it quick before people start — getting really sick." She shivered as she thought about Mark Cutter and his family. "I've got to figure out some way to get in there myself."

"I'm sure you can do it. Oh, by the way, you asked me to find out about those True Light people. That religious group. A bunch of them, maybe twenty or so, lived on that property for two or three years. And they're *kaput,* Billie. All of them dead."

"Jesus Christ," she said. "That would mean —"

"It probably means, at the very least, there's some natural source of lodestar they got in the drinking water or maybe even through food, if they grew their own food on that land."

"Oh, shit!" she said under her breath. "So even if Spencer isn't giving them the stuff himself, they're still getting it. And Alice's baby granddaughter is out there."

Outside, the summer sun blazed down on Alice Cutter's house overlooking the James River.

* * * * *

Twenty miles to the west, in the office of the commune, Dexter Spencer's temper blazed equally hot on Worthington French. "What in hell do you mean, you don't know what it is?" Spencer raged as he looked over Worth French's shoulder at the report he had spread out on the table, the Atlas Chemicals logo at the top of each page.

Spencer's tone angered French. "Look here,

Dexter, I can't help it if the fucking chemists at ACI say they've never seen anything like this goddamned stuff before."

"And you say that means we can't make it synthetically?"

"We can't make it if we don't know what to put in it. The only thing we can do is mine it, like coal."

Spencer considered that for a few seconds. Then he said, "We're talking megabucks to put in an honest-to-God mining operation. Would ACI put up the cash?"

Frowning, French replied, "I told you up front we didn't have a lot of development money to play with. The answer is no. Besides, I would have to get approval from the ACI board to spend that kind of money, and frankly, I don't want them to know about this . . . substance."

"What you mean is," Spencer said, "that if ACI puts up the money, ACI gets the profit."

French blushed down to his collar, then stammered, "There must be another way."

Considering the possibility, Spencer nodded slowly. "I think there is, but it would involve some risk. I hadn't planned to use the stuff on anyone and send them off the commune. At least not yet. But Roger Plank is one of our members *and* the vice-president of the First Commonwealth Bank. He could get the money for us."

"A loan?"

"Goddamn it, Worth, no! Don't be stupid! That would mean paperwork up the yin-yang and financial declarations and all that kind of shit. Besides, this place is mortgaged to the hilt and I happen to know you're on the verge of personal bankruptcy."

French blanched. He hoped that was all Spencer knew. "What are you thinking, Dexter?" he said.

"I'm thinking that Roger Plank can waltz into that bank and just take the money. He can fix it on the books."

"But *if* he were caught and *if* anybody discovered our role in this, they'd dump us both in prison and let us rot!" French drew himself up piously.

"Spare me the act, Worth. You didn't get where you are without a few crooked deals. And we stand a chance to earn millions with this stuff when it's for sale on the international market."

French erupted. "I thought you intended to sell it to *our* government. To sell it elsewhere would be treason!"

"Probably." Spencer's hard, black eyes expressed disdain for the businessman's caution. "But hell, it's not much different from when the U.S. sells weapons to other countries who could conceivably turn them back on us, now is it? And they do that all the time, French. Haven't you ever heard of the capitalist ethic? A buck before honor?"

They stared at one another like two pit bulls squaring off. Finally Spencer said, "Will you help me in this? I still need your company's name, if not its financial backing."

French struggled with the decision for a few moments, then seemed to wilt in body and in spirit as he made up his mind. "All right. I'll help you. But I don't like it."

"Good man," Spencer said with obvious relief. "We'll send Plank after the money tomorrow."

* * * * *

Odell Munsington had built himself a small distillation apparatus in the woods, not too far from the lake. Since his limited success with Maxie, his mind seemed to have gone out of control on him. All he could think about was sex and the possibilities that the *lake magic* (as he had begun to call the stuff in his head) opened up to him.

Every day he visited the still to collect the few grains of the magic that were produced overnight and to refill the distillation tank with lake water. By this time, he had about a half-tablespoon of it in a plastic bag.

He whistled happily as he finished refilling the water in the still, stuffed the baggie with the lake magic in his pocket and headed for the chapel. Perhaps if he spent an hour or so in prayer, he would feel even better.

* * * * *

Stephanie had a tall tumbler of Scotch in her hand when she answered her front door about seven-thirty that night.

"Who is it?" she asked cautiously.

When a woman's voice answered, she opened the door.

Megan Cameron pushed her roughly aside and flounced into the house. "I have to talk to you," she nearly screamed. She was sobbing and seemed about to hyperventilate.

Stephanie led her to the den. "Calm down," she told her. "Let me fix you a drink."

"*You* calm down, you *bitch!* Robin told me everything! You've got a lot of nerve. Seeing me as a patient and then sleeping with my girlfriend. I'm going to file charges against you for unethical behavior!"

"I don't consider you my patient. The only reason I saw you at all was to make a referral." On the surface, Stephanie was unruffled, but tiny little cold fingers of anxiety were running up and down her spine.

Megan ignored her denial. "And how dare you suggest to Robin that I'm making things up! What the hell are you trying to do, make her think I'm crazy so you can get your grubby little hands on her? Well, it's not going to work, do you hear me? *It's not going to work!*" The veins in her neck looked like they might burst. She swiped at her nose with a hand.

Stephanie blinked at her. "What are you talking about, Megan?" she said evenly.

"You *must* have told her that! Why else would she accuse me of sending those notes to myself?"

"What?" Stephanie said incredulously.

Just as suddenly as she had come in, Megan headed back for the front door, her high heels clicking and her full skirt swaying with her unsteady gait. She had delivered her message. Now she could leave. She stopped on the porch for one final attack. "If you ever try to see Robin again, *Doctor* Scott, much less *screw* her, I'm going to *kill* you! I'll bust your ass from here to Texas. You get that through your scheming little head! I've done it before. I will not have you ruining our life —"

A hail of bullets smacked into the front of the house, sending splinters and brick fragments everywhere.

Stephanie yelled, "Get down!" She dropped to the floor as she heard a cry of pain. Then she heard the thud of Megan's falling body.

An engine started, backfired, then smoothed out evenly. A car pulled away from the curb with a screech of tires. Then silence.

Stephanie crawled to the phone in the den and called the police.

* * * * *

Alice Cutter stood ramrod straight in the center of the kitchen floor. The clock above the stove said nine-fifteen.

"Do you understand what I'm telling you, Alice?" Billie asked her. She stubbed out her Marlboro and brushed at the ashes on her sleeve.

"I understand. My worst fears for Mark and his family are true. Something is horribly wrong at Enlightenment. And you're not going to tell me what it is."

In her mind, Billie cursed the FBI's need for secrecy. If only she could explain to Alice about the lodestar. But King had said it was for her ears only, and lover or not, she could not tell Alice the truth.

"You have to trust me on this, sweetheart. I'd tell you all I know if I could. The important thing is we have to get Mark and Ruth and the baby out of there immediately. I'm going after them tomorrow. I'd go now, but there are some preparations I have to make."

"What if they won't come with you? Mark believes so strongly in the man, Billie. He kept saying over and over that what Spencer tells him to do is good for him. That it's for everybody's good. Mark believes it."

"They'll come. I'll see to that. Have I ever lied to you?"

"Never."

"Then believe that I will get Alicia and her mom and dad out of there safely. Alice, if you love me, trust me."

"You mean that, don't you? You'll get them?"

"I've never lied to you, Alice. Sometimes I can't tell you the whole truth. Like now. And I'm sorry for that. It just has to be."

"I know," Alice said with resignation. "And I didn't mean to imply that I don't trust you. I do. I just . . ."

Billie put her finger on Alice's lips. "You go to bed now. And go to sleep. I have a few phone calls to make."

But in spite of her trust in Billie, Alice knew she would lay awake most of the night.

* * * * *

Robin Oakley sat in the emergency room waiting to hear about Megan's condition. Stephanie sat beside her, numb with shock. "Wonder what's taking so long," Stephanie said.

Robin frowned as if she didn't understand the words. Robin was royally drunk. "Goddamn it, Stephie! I don't know what got into me." She paused and pulled at her ear. "Yes, I do. It was the booze. See they had this party after work for this guy who's being transferred, and everybody was drinking and — anyway, when I got home, I just told her."

131

"You told her we — made love?"

Robin sighed, then squinted as she tried to think clearly. "I told her that. And I told her the other thing too."

"You told her what other thing? Drink your coffee." She had bought two large-sized cups from the vending machine.

"About how I had figured it out. That she had to be making all this up. The phone calls stopped when we put the wiretap on. How could the rapist have known we tapped the phone? And nobody *anywhere,*" she drew out the word for at least five seconds, ". . . saw the car she said she was picked up in. *But,* she said he let her out at a service station in broad daylight. A-n-nnd, the *really* funny thing is, we've had an off-duty-cop watching the house all the time for days, and guess what?"

"What?" Stephanie said, lamely playing along with Robin.

"Nobody's been to the mailbox but Megan and me. And two more notes have arrived. So I figured she must have put them there. I sure as hell didn't."

"What about the mailman?"

"What *about* the mailman?" Robin parroted drunkenly.

"Couldn't he be the one leaving the notes?"

"The mailman is a mailwoman. Why do you always think in stereotypes, Stephanie?" Robin slapped her knee and laughed uproariously at her own wit.

"Drink your coffee," Stephanie said again. "Robin, how long did you know Megan before she moved in with you?"

"Correction. I moved in with her. She's the one

with all the money. You know cops don't make that kind of dough. She bought that house. Cost her a couple of hundred thousand. And I had known her about a month."

"So you really don't know much about her?"

"I know somebody tried to kill her tonight. So maybe I was wrong about her doing those things herself."

Stephanie said, "Did it ever occur to you, Miss Self-Absorbed, that *I* might have been the intended victim of this shooting? Megan looks an awful lot like me, in case you hadn't noticed."

"You? Why who —" Robin suddenly sobered. "That Rooney fellow!"

Stephanie was trying not to show she was scared. "I just hope *somebody* in the neighborhood saw the car. It must have been parked down the block. It all happened so fast."

"Well, Les Knight has people canvassing the area. If anybody saw it, we'll know soon." She looked at her feet for a long while. "And he's also running a check on Megan's background. The truth is, I don't know shit about her. She may not even be from North Carolina, for all I know . . ." Her voice trailed off and she took a long drink of the coffee.

The door to the waiting area snapped open. "Robin Oakley?" The voice belonged to a wiry man in scrub greens. A stethoscope hung from his pocket.

"Over here." Robin weaved slightly as she stood up.

"I'm Dr. Brumley. Your friend is going to be okay. The wound was made by a shotgun, as you perhaps already know. The shot was very fine, like people often use to shoot birds. It's taken us all this

133

time to dig about a thousand tiny pellets out of her back and buttocks. She's going to be sore and we'll keep her overnight for observation, but you can take her home tomorrow. Okay? Any questions?"

"How is she? Can I see her?" Robin asked shakily.

"She's sleepy from the anesthetic, but you can go in for a few minutes. Just don't stay long." He walked quickly back through the doors to the ER.

"No. No, I won't stay," she said to his back. "Stephanie, I —"

"You go ahead and see her, Robin. But just so we understand each other, this doesn't change a thing. I still want you to leave me alone."

Stephanie wheeled around and headed for the door.

CHAPTER NINE

The moon was already down at three o'clock in the morning. In the distance, Billie heard a thunderstorm growling. The sunrise would probably be dulled by the rain. She tested the unfamiliar car's windshield wipers to make sure they were in working order.

She had laid out the details of her plan to Phil King the night before as if it were a foregone conclusion that Phil would do precisely what she told him to. She would accept no alternatives in strategy simply because there was no time to consider other courses of action. Every fiber of her being kept giving her the same message: *Time is running out for Alicia Cutter.* Maybe time was running out for Mark and Ruth too, but it was an undebatable fact that if Alice's grandbaby was being exposed to lodestar, her days were numbered. Perhaps even her hours.

The tires of the Virginia Highway Patrol car made a whining sound on the macadam roadway as she wound her way through the backwoods toward Enlightenment. The uniform she wore was dark blue with gold trim. The sleeves bore the Commonwealth of Virginia seal. Beside her on the seat was the traditional Smokey Bear hat.

The high beams of the vehicle impaled the summer night mist like a lighthouse beacon. A rickety roadside sign up ahead leaped up like a ghost as the lights suddenly struck it. The sign announced in faded letters: COLONIAL CAMPGROUND ELECTRIC AND WATER HOOK-UPS $8 A NIGHT NO PETS NEXT RIGHT.

She drove on, depending on her reflexes, as she let her mind slip back to another night and another campground. Her mother's voice seemed to come out of the night from nowhere, everywhere.

"Billie, Billie, don't. Don't cry."

Her memory's keen eye could still see the worn-out, rust-streaked Winnebago they had lived in. How long? God knew. The days of a six-year-old little girl are longer than most; and the hurts of being alive and poor sting harder and deeper.

Her mother had taken her in her arms that night and rocked her, kissing her now and then on her tightly braided hair. "I love you," she had crooned. "I wouldn't ask you to do it if there was any other way. We got no money, Billie."

Billie's precocious mind had known that was true. Her father had taken off one night in Arkansas. Just left without so much as a kiss my ass. They had made it to Kentucky, headed back to her mother's home in West Virginia. But the money had run out and her mother had not found work.

"But it's wrong, Mama. And I get so scared. What if they catch me?" She rubbed at her leaky nose with her small fist.

"What would they do to you if they did?" her mother said, trying hard to soothe her. "A pretty and brave little angel like you? All you gotta do is just crawl in that little window in the camp store and bring out whatever food you can carry. There ain't nobody there at night. Never is in these campgrounds."

Billie had done it, as she had done it before and would do it again other nights. And she had made a solemn vow that someday she would make it up to the world, all that stealing. It had been a small thing. Just a few groceries. But to her little girl's heart, it had mattered. It had mattered a lot.

She took the dirt road that went straight on to Enlightenment. Deep ruts were developing. The light mist of rain that had begun wouldn't help them any, she thought, as blue lightning flashed like greedy fingers across the distant sky.

The headlights found the closed farm gate and the car rocked on its springs as she stopped sharply. She played the patrol car's spotlight over the gate.

Chained and padlocked. She took the stiff-brimmed hat from the seat, unsnapped the leather strap across her service revolver and got out of the car.

She stood by the fence for a moment, trying to decide whether to pick the lock or cut the chain with the bolt cutters in the trunk. Too late she heard the click of a rifle bolt. She turned to face the sound.

"Something I can do for you, Officer?"

"No need for that," she said, pointing toward the rifle barrel.

"Whatcha doin' out here in the middle of the night?" the man asked, his reedy voice none too friendly.

As Billie squinted at him through the car lights, another bolt of lightning lit up the sky so that she could see him clearly for a moment. He looked rather ordinary. About six feet tall. Longish brown unkempt hair. White cotton undershirt over brown Levis. He was wearing black high-top tennis shoes, one of them untied.

"I'm Officer Robinson," she said, pointing to the gold-plated name tag on her shirt. "I need to see Mark Cutter and his wife right away. Open the gate."

"Didn't think Virginia hired no women on the patrol," the man said. "Maybe you rented that monkey suit for some kinda party?"

"Yes, sir, they do hire women. Now if you could just open the gate . . ."

"Can't do that. Got orders not to let nobody in unless Mr. Spencer tells me." He lifted the rifle to his shoulder. "You ain't no exception."

Shit. The man was going to give her a hard time. She touched her own gun lightly.

"Look, fella, this is an emergency. And put the damned rifle down. Don't you know it's a crime to point a gun at an officer of the law?"

He lowered the gun slightly. "What kind of emergency?"

Billie walked toward the driver's side of the car as she talked. "That's none of your business, buster. Now I'm going through that gate, whether you open it or not. You want to do it the easy way or the hard way? It's up to you. But you fire that rifle at me and you've got twenty years — even if you don't hit me."

The man moved the beam of his flashlight over her face as she got into the car and cranked the engine. "Five seconds," she said, "and I'm going through that goddamned fence. And I'm going to arrest you for obstructing justice when I come back. You got that, dickface?"

He read the resolution in her eyes. Dexter Spencer would kick his royal ass if he called him in the middle of the night, but still, woman or not, he believed she *was* an officer. He raised the walkie-talkie so that he was sure she could see it.

"I have to call the boss," he said.

"You do that — when you see the glow of my taillights! Now open the damned gate or I'm going through it!"

He did as he was told.

Billie gunned the engine hard and left him a face full of mud.

* * * * *

139

It had taken Megan a few hours to regain enough consciousness to realize that she was in a hospital. It had taken her fifteen minutes more to realize she had to get out. She had long since had her fill of hospitals. Fucking hospitals with their barred windows and their damned shock treatments. Two-faced nurses with their *oh we have to take our medicine* routine. What a crock of shit!

Busy with the chores that fend off the boredom of the night shift, none of the nurses even noticed when Megan crept out of her room fully dressed. Little by little, hiding in the night shadows, she made it to the first floor. From there it would be easy. She'd just square up her shoulders and walk toward the door as if it were the most normal thing in the world to do at four o'clock in the morning. Her shoulders and back felt sore, but she tried hard not to show it as she moved toward the entrance.

The pink lady at the reception desk by the door looked up from the book she was reading as Megan approached. "What are you doing, young lady?" she said indignantly. "You can't leave here in the middle of the night. You can't be a nurse. The nursing shift doesn't end until six. Show me your identification."

The voice stopped Megan as if she had walked into an invisible barrier. She swayed slightly from side to side. "You can't stop me," she hissed through clenched teeth.

"I can call the guard."

As the woman made a move toward the phone, Megan lifted her purse high over her head, then brought it down hard. The woman's head cracked loudly as it struck the desk. Megan pushed open the door and ran into the street.

The night air felt fresh on her face, and she took a deep breath to clear her head. She thought she would feel even better if the voices would leave her alone. Would be fine, in fact, if they would just be quiet. But the voices had been whispering for some time now. For days, it seemed, but so low she could barely hear them.

Downtown Richmond spread out before her, deserted except for an occasional set of car lights flashing up Broad Street. She supposed she would have to walk wherever she was going. There would probably be no cabs this time of night. She felt in her pockets but came up with no money. Not even a quarter for a phone call. The feeling of being totally alone flooded her chest. Suddenly she couldn't stop shaking.

The wind was picking up and whistled loudly as it whipped around the corners of office buildings. Clouds were sweeping across the sky, racing like enormous gray ghosts set on crossing some far, unseen finish line.

Unsummoned memories crowded her mind. Sharp, painful memories that, once unleashed, came at her like a pack of wild dogs set on tearing her apart. At first she saw her mother, coming at her with a stick, a fire poker, grinning like she was deranged. Then the figure changed, fading into the dark shape of her stepfather, standing over her, drunk and cursing, angry and taking swipes at her with huge bony hands. Striking her hard with his fists. Then touching her where he shouldn't touch, even as she fought him as hard as she could.

BOOM. BOOM. Thunder rattled in the distance. BLOOD, BAD, KILL, MURDER. Had the words come

141

from the thunder or inside her brain? Megan shook her head to clear it.

Got to get home to Robin, she thought with sudden clarity, and she began to run.

Maybe Robin could still the voices. Maybe Robin could stop her before she — what? Her brain was not willing to end the thought. All she knew was that she had to get home. Fast.

* * * * *

A clap of thunder echoed through the night, and the wind seemed to gain strength in the wake of the noise. As if poured from a bucket, rain flooded the windshield of the patrol car, making the windshield wipers nearly worthless. Brilliant explosions of lightning lit up the terrain, giving the world a stroboscopic look and a feeling of unreality.

Billie Robinson braked and turned sharply into the parking lot at the Enlightenment office. The patrol car took the corner smoothly, sliding only slightly in the mud. The place looked just as Alice had described it.

She parked near the front of the lot, and took a large flashlight from the back seat. Quickly she pulled on a yellow slicker before she flashed a beam of light over the dark building. In the storm, an air of menace hung over the place. Billie shivered as it occurred to her that this building might hold sinister secrets capable of drastically changing the fate of the world.

She was about to move toward the front door

when headlights appeared in the darkness and a Chevy Blazer pulled in behind her. It stopped a few inches from where she was standing.

Billie put her hand against the front fender and frowned as she raised the beam of the light to flood the interior of the vehicle. At first she didn't recognize him, but when he rolled down the window, she saw that it was Dexter Spencer. The scrubby beard and dark eyes were familiar from the picture in his file.

"What is it, Officer?" Spencer said. His face showed no emotion when Billie moved to the side of the car and swept the Blazer's inside with the flashlight. But she could feel him study her face intently.

"You run this place?" she asked him.

"God runs this place," he said. "I am just the physical body that carries out his work."

"You don't say," she said and moved the beam to his face. "You're Dexter Spencer, aren't you?"

Spencer looked surprised. "You know me?" he asked.

"No," she said. "But I know of you."

"Yes, well," he mumbled. "A lot of people know of our good work here at Enlightenment. No matter. How can I help you, Officer?"

Thunder rumbled, but softer. Not like the explosions that had shaken the air a few minutes before. Billie considered telling him she knew more about him than his so-called good works, then thought better of it. All she needed now was his cooperation. The rest would come in time.

"I need to see Mark Cutter," she answered.

"In the middle of the night? Why, Officer, you can't expect —"

Billie held up her hand to silence him. "His mother has been injured in a car accident. I've come to take him to her."

"He won't go with you," Spencer said flatly, knowing Mark would do whatever he told him to do.

"I think that should be his choice, don't you?"

Spencer said nothing for a moment. He couldn't afford to have the police think he was hiding something, but he didn't want Mark Cutter to leave Enlightenment either. If Mark's mother had her way, he'd never return. If she had much time with him, the old bitch might even figure out a way to take back the property Mark had signed over.

Billie waited patiently, listening to the rain beating on the car and the swish of the wipers. A steady rivulet of water ran from her hat and onto the side of the Blazer.

"No, he won't go," Spencer said firmly. "Mark is . . . is . . . sick. And his little girl is sick too. There's no way they can leave. Especially in the middle of a storm. He can come later. When they're well again."

Billie smiled into the darkness, knowing Spencer couldn't see her face. The man was sweating. She could almost smell it. Whatever was going on here, Spencer didn't want Mark Cutter to be free to tell about it. She decided to turn the heat up a little.

"Mr. Spencer," she began. "I'm getting the distinct impression that you don't want me to see Mark Cutter. You know, if the police had reason to believe you are holding anyone here against their will —"

"No, no," Spencer sputtered. "Nothing like that. I'm just . . . just concerned for the health of my friends."

"And there's a rumor, Mr. Spencer, that you might even be taking money from people in some kind of scam. If the police decided to take a look at your financial records —"

"No, no," Spencer almost shouted above the rain. "I'm just a businessman. An honest businessman. No need to —"

"Besides that, Mr. Spencer, I have a search warrant in my pocket here, and if you don't take me to the Cutters right now — and I mean *right now* — I'm going to handcuff you to that steering wheel and search the place. And I'll call in another half-dozen patrolmen to help me. No telling what we might find. You got that?" She opened her coat and touched her pistol to reinforce the idea that she meant business.

Spencer closed his eyes and swallowed. He couldn't have police all over the place. He'd just have to do as much reprogramming of the Cutters as he could manage in the short time he would have. After all, they would remember nothing except what he told them to remember. And if he lost Mark to his mother — well, better that than to lose everything.

"You got that?" Billie repeated. She made a move as if to draw her gun.

"No need, Officer," Spencer said quickly. "No need for all that. You wait here. I'll drive over to the

Cutters' cabin and give them the bad news. They'll need to take a few things. I'll help them pack, then bring them back here."

Some dark part of Billie briefly felt something like disappointment when he gave in so easily. She would have taken satisfaction from really humiliating this scumbag. But getting Alice's family to safety was her top priority. She could not afford to spend any more time arguing with the man.

"Then you get them, and get them fast," she said. "If you're not back here within the hour, I'll come after them myself. You hear?"

"I hear," Spencer said. He threw the vehicle into reverse and scowled at her through the wet windshield. "Fuck you," he said out loud as he pulled away from the office building.

CHAPTER TEN

Stephanie was still shaky as she dressed for work the next morning. She jumped when the doorbell rang. Maybe it was the man she had called to repair the damage caused by the gunshot.

But the man standing on her porch was not the repairman. "I'm Detective Knight, Dr. Scott," he said. "I don't wish to impose on you, but may I come in a moment? I, ah, I work with your friend Robin Oakley."

A look of surprise crossed Stephanie's face, for if

the man had not been black, he would have been a dead ringer for TV's Detective Columbo. Sloppy coat, rounded shoulders, cigar and all. And although Robin had mentioned the man numerous times, Stephanie had never seen him.

"I only have a few minutes before I must leave for work."

"This shouldn't take too long," he said.

As he sat down in the den, he put on a pair of half-moon reading glasses and looked at his notes. "Now Dr. Scott, we picked Greg Rooney up this morning. One of our cruisers spotted his car parked at a 7-Eleven. The gun was in the trunk."

"Thank heaven!" Stephanie said. "I'm so relieved! I think that gunshot last night was meant for me."

"Yes, ma'am, it was."

"You're sure?"

"Yes, ma'am. One of your neighbors wrote down the license number of the car as it left your block after the shooting. But you won't have to worry about him anymore."

Stephanie breathed a sigh of relief, then remembered. "The children? Have you found the children?"

"Rooney's been staying in a trailer park out on Jefferson Davis Highway. Had their card in his wallet. The children were there. Scared, but okay."

"Thank God," Stephanie said.

"Yes, ma'am. I thought you also should know that Megan Cameron left the hospital last night. On her own. In the middle of the night. Would you have any idea why she might do that?"

Stephanie was astonished. "The only thing I can

think of is that she was upset when she came to see me. She and . . . a friend had had some kind of argument."

"Dr. Scott," Les Knight said. "You don't need to be vague with me. I know all about her relationship with Robin Oakley. And I know about Robin's relationship with you. Police officers get pretty close to each other. It doesn't matter to me that you're gay. So don't hold out on me."

Is there anybody left in the world who doesn't know, she thought idly. Stephanie eyed him gravely, then decided she might as well be honest with him. "Well," she began, "she was pretty put out with Robin and she did threaten me. Just before the gunshot. But I don't think she'd . . ."

"Threatened you how?"

Stephanie hesitated. "Detective, I don't really think she meant it, but she said she would kill me if I saw Robin again."

"Kill you." He scribbled that down in his notebook. "But you don't believe she meant it." He scribbled again.

"Robin said you were looking into her background."

"Yes, ma'am. And if there's anything to know, we'll find it. Something's out of whack with that woman."

"You don't believe anyone has been threatening her? Robin didn't believe it until the shooting."

"No, ma'am, I don't. I haven't for some time. But I was waiting for Robin to catch on before I said anything. Don't think she'd have taken it too kindly if I'd suggested that her girlfriend was a kook."

"A kook? You don't think Robin would get involved with a — someone who was seriously disturbed, do you?"

Knight opened his mouth to speak. Then shut it. Then came out with what he was thinking anyway. "If you don't mind my saying so, Dr. Scott, Robin was pretty busted up when the two of you split. She didn't say anything, but I could tell. She and I have been partners off and on for a long time. As they say back in Georgia where I come from, she hasn't known her ass from a hole in the ground since she left this house."

She blushed a bright scarlet. "Yes, well, Robin is often impetuous."

"Big word," he said, lifting his bushy eyebrows. His dark eyes had a peculiar gleam in them. "If you mean she leaps before she looks, she doesn't. Not usually. But you put her between a rock and a hard place, Dr. Scott. Robin loves police work. You know, of course, that her father and her grandfather were policemen. She's carrying on the family tradition. You asked her to give that up and she couldn't. So she left you so you wouldn't have to worry about her so much. Not because she had stopped caring about you."

Stephanie sat silent. Finally she said, "If that's all, Detective, I really do have to leave for work."

He stood up to go. "I guess I've overstepped my bounds and I hope you'll forgive me for that."

"No problem," she said, unconvincingly.

As he closed the screen door behind him, he turned. "You be careful, you hear?"

The words struck her like a blow to the stomach.

Andrew Brown had told her the same thing about Greg Rooney.

And Greg Rooney had tried to shoot her.

* * * * *

The waiting room at the National Institutes of Health hospital in Bethesda, Maryland, was aseptic-looking. Plain to a fault. The walls were pale green, the furniture simple and uncomfortable. There were no magazines and no ashtrays. Not even any plastic flowers. The two large paintings were abstracts done in monotonous earth tones.

Alice Cutter sat very still on one of the stiff sofas. She looked pale and drawn. Billie Robinson paced the floor. They had arrived by agency helicopter an hour before. They were waiting for the doctor who was examining the young Cutter family. When Dr. Sam Plyler came out, he looked so tired and frazzled that it was hard to place a great deal of confidence in him.

Alice rose. She searched his face expectantly. He was small and round-shouldered, as if his burden in life was almost too much for him. He was badly in need of a shave; his blond beard glistened in the fluorescent lighting. When he spoke his voice was soft and it was clear that he was genuinely concerned. And competent.

"Good morning, Mrs. Cutter. First I want to tell you that it was good that you got them here when you did," he began. "Especially the baby."

"Will they be all right?" Alice asked in a fearful voice.

"Mark and Ruth, I can tell you about now. It's clear they have ingested — probably ingested," he corrected himself, "some kind of poison. Each of them is showing an indication of liver impairment but it is slight. But yes. As long as they rest and have a good diet, they should be okay. The liver is an interesting organ. It will repair itself if not damaged too severely."

"And little Alicia?" Alice shuddered, unwilling to put words to what she was thinking.

"I have to be honest with you, Mrs. Cutter. The little tyke's not in great shape now. She's already beginning to show jaundice. Our plan is to put her on a treatment plan which involves —"

"I don't care what kind of treatment you use, Doctor!" Alice blurted impatiently. "Just tell me if she'll be all right!"

Dr. Plyler showed no visible reaction to the outburst. "To tell you the truth, we don't know yet. She's an awfully little girl. We'll just have to hope and pray for the best. If she's a fighter, there's a good chance she'll be fine."

"Can I see her?"

"She's resting now. Asleep probably. I'd rather not have her disturbed at the moment. But tomorrow evening, during visiting hours, you'll be able to see her. You can see your son and daughter-in-law now if you want to."

He took her hand and patted it. Then he turned and walked at a fast clip across the lounge.

Billie circled Alice's shoulders with her arm. "She's a strong baby. She's like her grandmother. She'll be okay."

"I don't feel so strong right now."

"And understandably so. You need some rest too. I've rented a room for you. It's only a block from here. You can walk back over here in the morning to see them. Go on and look in on Mark and Ruth for a few minutes. Explain to them, if you can, why we had to tell them what we did about your being in an accident. I have to make a phone call, then I'll take you to your room so you can get some sleep."

"Are you going to stay with me?"

"I would if I could, but I have to get back to Richmond. This thing with Enlightenment has to be finished."

"I love you," Alice said.

"Love you, too. Now go on and see Mark."

* * * * *

One hundred and fifty miles to the southwest, the dawn had pushed away an ebony sky. The drizzle of rain falling near the capital of the Confederacy left the morning a muted gray.

Odell Munsington knocked tentatively, then loudly on the door of Maxie's living quarters. He had used all the stealth he could muster to drop half the "lake magic" he had collected into her drinking water at dinner. During the night he had undressed her and had sex with her a dozen times in his head. He had talked himself out of actually doing it a dozen times more, but his passion had finally exceeded his good sense. Now he stood trembling at her door. Not with fear, but anticipation.

"Let me in," he said when she appeared. Her

blonde hair was tousled from sleep. The T-shirt she wore barely covered her underpants. She scrubbed sleepily at her eyes. Then she pushed open the door.

He stepped past her into the rustic cabin. The walls and floors were made of unfinished boards, the ceiling of open beams. Besides a chest of drawers and a wash stand, there was only the bunk bed. The blue and white striped bedspread lay in a crumpled heap. The top bunk was covered with cast-aside clothing. The thin window shades were pulled against the early morning sun.

"You have a roommate?" he asked her.

"No."

"Expecting anyone?" He didn't know if any of the single commune members ever slept together, but he would take no chances of being interrupted this time.

"No one."

"Close the door."

She did as she was told. Then waited for his instruction.

For several moments, he appraised her body. She was not as young as he had first imagined, but she was a juicy morsel, even in her clothes. His mouth watered. And he could make her do anything he wanted. No matter how vile or how perverse the act. And no one would ever know. He felt his male organ swell in size at the thought.

"Is there something else you want?" she asked him.

"No. Yes! Take off your shirt. I want to see you naked."

With her arms over her head, her breasts seemed average sized, but when she lowered them, the

154

breasts seemed to Munsington to bloom. They were large. With dark, smooth nipples. Momentarily, he wondered if she bleached her hair.

"Now your panties."

She stripped them off and kicked them away from her. Her dark curly mound confirmed his suspicions about the hair.

"Nice," he murmured. "Now lean back on the bed."

She backed away from him until her calves struck the mattress, then she sat down.

"Lean back, I said."

She did as she was told and waited.

"Start rubbing your nipples. Do it so I can see."

Very lightly, she placed her flattened hand over her breast and began a slow, circular movement. The nipple swelled and strained.

"Good. Great," he whispered. This was better than all the porn movies he had ever seen. God! What power to be the director of such things! His mind raced over the possibilities of what he might ask her to do and he felt his knees buckle slightly.

"Maxie, I want you to play with yourself. Enjoy it!"

She tried to comply, rubbing her breasts slowly and deliberately, but an expression of extreme distress was on her face.

Munsington didn't seem to notice. He slowly unzipped his fly.

Oh great God, the power! he thought. Praise God! The power! Then he could contain himself no longer. He grabbed at his crotch and began to massage himself. Power! Power! Penis power! The words echoed through his brain like some primitive chant and blocked out all reason. When he freed his phallus, it stuck out like a huge purple club. His eyes glazed over as he grabbed himself roughly and walked toward Maxie.

"Say you want me," he grunted.

"I want you," she muttered.

"Say you're so hot you can't stand it."

"Hot!" she groaned. She made a low throaty noise. Like strangling. Then quite suddenly, she relaxed and lay unmoving like a rag doll. Her complexion had gone pasty white.

Munsington stood over her and stroked himself impatiently. "Open your legs," he demanded.

Maxie did not move. Instead her glassy, lifeless eyes stared up at him.

"Maxie! Do what I tell you. Open your legs!"

When she did not move, Munsington reached to part her legs with a chubby hand. He knelt over the woman, his face flushed and body trembling. He licked his lips. "Maxie?" he said, panting. "Do what I tell you!"

When the woman lay still, he grabbed her harshly by the arm and shook her. "You little bitch!" he screamed at her. "You do what I tell you!"

He pulled her up roughly from the bed, then thrust her away from him. The sight of her limp body seemed first to infuriate him, then to mesmerize him, so that he failed to hear the door open behind him.

But when the voice rang out — *Odell! What in the shit are you doing!* — his penis melted like a stick of butter. He turned to face the hard eyes of Dexter Spencer.

156

CHAPTER ELEVEN

The morning air in the main building at Enlightenment was heavy and humid. Rain beat on the broad window that overlooked the lake leaving tiny beads, like teardrops, that broke and coursed downward.

Dexter Spencer stood looking out. Waiting. His hands were drawn into fists, his teeth clenched so hard that the jaw muscles in his bony face jutted out like a chipmunk's.

Odell sat in one of the high-backed chairs, his face clouded with contrition. The skin on his forehead shone with slick sweat. Dexter had not allowed him to speak for the past twenty minutes. Periodically he fidgeted, then stopped abruptly when Spencer glared at him.

When the door burst open and Worth French entered, he was breathless and his impatience showed in jerky movements. "I came as soon as I could. What's the situation here, Dexter? You said it was urgent."

Spencer turned to face him. There was a revolver tucked into his belt. "Things have changed, my dear French." He pointed to Munsington, who studied his feet. "We have to make some plans about what to do with this asshole here. I didn't want to do anything . . . drastic without consulting you."

"What the hell are you talking about? And what are you doing with that damned gun?" French pulled nervously at the knot in his silk tie.

"This blockhead has been distilling the chemicals out of the lake and using the stuff . . . for sex . . . to get women to have sex with him. I found a bag of it in his pocket. And I caught him doing . . . obscene things with one of the girls."

French sat down at the table and glared, first at one man, then the other. He sucked in his breath. "That's the most insane thing I've ever heard!"

"Isn't it? Here we are, sitting on a motherfucking gold mine, and this bastard can't pass up a piece of tail! We have the opportunity of a lifetime, a chance to own the world if we want it and this idiot, this superdick . . ." Spencer sputtered and choked on his own fury.

"It was a mistake. I . . . I . . . I apologize." Munsington stuttered, his head on his chest.

"It was a disaster, you lunatic!" Spencer spat at him. His face had turned a delicate shade of purple. "What if somebody besides me had walked in on you? You're *supposed* to be the goddamned spiritual leader at this place! You're *supposed* to have repented for all your past sins! What do you want people to think, that we're running a fucking whorehouse up here? Don't you know the authorities would shut us down? They'd do it in a heartbeat! That girl you . . . molested was sixteen years old!"

"I'm sorry," Munsington said lamely. "I won't do it again."

"Sorry? Sorry! You idiot! You bet your dick you're sorry! That girl is dead! You hear me? Fucking dead! Can't you get that through your thick skull?"

French went green around the mouth. "Dead? Dead? What happened here, Spencer? Did he kill somebody? Who did he kill?"

"I don't know what happened," Spencer said sourly. "He says he didn't do anything to her except — except tell her to stroke her own body while he watched. If that's true, it was probably the drug that killed her."

"Oh Lord," French said. "How much of it did he give her?"

Spencer pitched the plastic bag he had taken from Munsington onto the table. "He says about half that much."

French shook his head. "That would certainly be enough to kill her. I just finished running the dose response curves on the rats last night. The stuff is definitely lethal at high doses."

"Shit!" Spencer yelled. He pounded the table. "Shit! Shit! Shit!"

"Get a hold on yourself, Dexter," French said sternly. "We have to think. Is there any way this will pass for death by natural causes? Maybe suicide? Did she use drugs?"

"The best thing is probably just to notify the authorities that she ran away. Lots of teenagers do it," Spencer suggested.

"And her body? What will we do with it?" French asked.

"Maybe we'll bury it in the woods. I'll make this asshole do it himself."

French considered that for only a moment, then said with resignation, "That seems like the only thing we *can* do. Now what about your banker, Plank? If we don't get started soon —"

"I've been working on Plank for a couple of days. I think he's ready. Just a few tests I want to put him through yet to be sure he will obey me even after he's out of my sight. And you're right, we have to get the money and get started. Now. Especially after this." He gestured disgustedly toward Munsington.

"I don't like all this," French grumbled. "I have an awful feeling everything is about to blow up in our faces."

"You think I like it?" Spencer challenged him with his black eyes. "You want out? You can still get out. I can find somebody else who wants to be a millionaire."

French was silent.

"I didn't think so. You just keep running your laboratory tests. If we could synthesize the stuff —"

160

Spencer's voice dropped lower, then rose again. "I'll take care of this mess here. I just thought you ought to know. It's your neck as well as mine."

"Yes," French muttered. "My neck too." As he stood up to leave, he had a sick feeling in the pit of his stomach that his life had gotten completely out of hand.

* * * * *

Billie Robinson ripped the headphones off when the door of the main building slammed behind Worth French. She had heard enough. The days and weeks of listening and recording had finally paid off. A smile of satisfaction crept across her face.

"Now doesn't that just take the cake," she said. "Worth French hooked up with that slimy Dexter Spencer."

Thank God Alice had finally remembered finding the Atlas Chemicals International pad and had mentioned it to her. If she hadn't already had Phil check out ACI and its officers, she would have had to wait for that report. And time was becoming a luxury she couldn't afford.

It all made sense. Spencer must have brought French in to help with the commercial production of the lodestar. And he had agreed because he desperately needed the money. It would seem that none of them at Enlightenment had realized the potential danger of the substance until now, and even if they had deliberately used it to manipulate people like Mark and Ruth — and she was sure in her heart that Spencer had — that could be hard to prove. The girl's death was really an accident. Spencer could always claim people were getting the stuff from the water or food and he didn't know it. He could say he just thought people were being inordinately generous. No. She'd need more proof. She wanted to nail him for good, with no loopholes for him to slip through.

She wished to God there was more evidence. She wanted to close the place down and arrest them all. Today. Right now. She was certain they were as guilty as sin, but she would have to be patient a little bit longer.

Billie sighed. Waiting seemed to be the prime occupation of FBI agents.

* * * * *

Mirrors.

They fascinated Robin Oakley. She'd always secretly wished she had nerve enough to install mirrors on the ceiling of her bedroom. Especially when she'd lived with Stephanie. But she'd never dared mention it for fear of being laughed at. Or worse than that, accused of being a narcissist. What was it Stephanie had called her? Miss Self-Absorbed?

She watched her reflection in the silver mirror over the bar as she fingered the rim of the glass that held her sixth drink — or was it the seventh — of the morning. She looked tired and not a little inebriated. She had not gone home when she left the hospital, making a conscious decision to spend her day off drinking herself into oblivion. And she had made a good start.

The place was a gay bar on Cary Street called Beebo's. A meeting place for the terminally lonely and the sexually horny of all ages.

For the most part, Robin hated gay bars. She was never at ease watching the young dykes with their freshly scrubbed faces and their strong limbs as they flirted and courted. They were undeniably appealing and beautiful in the dawn of their gay experience. But she always found herself wishing she could protect them all somehow from the mistakes she had made. From the pain of passion too often confused with love. From the never-fading confidence that the next love would be the last love. From the wounds inflicted by a homophobic society that promised it could be trusted, then stabbed viciously with a thousand little pieces of the broken mirror in which it saw lesbians reflected as some caricature of *real* human beings.

To Robin Oakley's eye, watching the older women in Beebo's was even worse. There was a desperation about them as they slouched at the bar or leaned across the tables, eyes sparkling too brightly, laughter a little too loud, a little drunk. Dark pits of unfulfilled wanting; deep gashes of unrequited longing. It was in the mirror of their eyes that Robin saw herself reflected. And it made her sad. "What the fuck," she said, and drank a toast to herself in the glass.

When the mirror reflected another face, the black face of Les Knight, Robin flinched. Before he could speak, she addressed him in a cranky tone. "I don't want to hear it, Les. Whatever it is, I *don't* want to hear it."

"Yes, you do. For one thing, we picked up Greg Rooney. He won't be bothering Stephanie any more."

"I hope you told her. She's not speaking to me ever again."

"I told her," he said. Then added, "Why don't you just bite off a piece of that glass and chew it up and swallow it, partner. That'll kill you a lot faster than that goddamned booze."

Robin didn't smile. Instead she took another deep swallow of the brown liquid. "You're not funny, Les. Why won't you just leave me alone? Give me another drink, Charlie," she yelled at the bartender.

"Put that damned stuff away!" Les said to Charlie as she approached with an open bottle of Virginia Gentleman. "I ought to arrest you for letting her get into this condition. Bring us some black coffee."

The bartender shrugged, reached under the counter and pulled out two stained white mugs.

Les sat down on the barstool beside Robin as Charlie poured steaming hot coffee. "I've been looking all over this damned city for you, woman. I have something to tell you and I want you to be able to understand it. Are you straight enough to listen?"

"Straight? Hell, no, I'm not straight! But then you know that, don't you, partner?" Her words were mildly slurred.

"Robin, you know I don't give a shit if you're

curved or zigzagged, I just don't want you to get hurt."

"So you say," she said, grinning sadly at their reflection in the mirror. "So don't hurt me then. Goodby, Lester."

"You listen to me, concrete head," Les said so softly she could barely hear him. "You might get hurt a lot worse if you don't listen. Robin, there is no record of a Megan Cameron in Winston-Salem, North Carolina. There never was. No school records. Nothing. I had the Winston police check back for forty years. They even checked the birth records for the whole state. No Megan Cameron."

"Don't tell me that crap. I saw her ID."

"Was it her driver's license?"

"Yeah. It had an address in Winston-Salem. Church Street or something."

"Maybe it was forged."

"It had her picture on it, for chrissakes!"

"That doesn't necessarily mean it was the real thing, my friend. The whole card could be a fake. It can be done."

"What the hell, Les? You think we're in some kind of James Bond movie? You've been watching too much fuckin' television!"

"Robin, she left the hospital. In the middle of the night, she just walked out."

Robin struggled to absorb the information without reacting. She concentrated on the bartender as she stuck a quarter in the jukebox. K.T. Oslin started bragging about eighties ladies.

"Is that a crime? Get the hell out of here, Les,"

Robin said finally. She knew Les was trying to help, but she just wanted to be left alone. She needed to process what he had said. If Megan wasn't Megan Cameron from North Carolina, who the hell was she? Why had she lied? And why had she run away?

"Well, she bopped some old lady on the head on her way out. That's a crime. Have you been home since you left the hospital last night?"

"No."

"Well, I have. I went by your house. Three or four times. She's not there."

"So what?" Robin blurted. "Maybe she left town. Jesus Christ, Les what do you want me to say? All right! I confess. I got myself involved with a woman that I know nothing about. I moved in with her because I was lonely. She's told lies about her life. Maybe she's tried to make it look like things were happening to her that were not. And now she's disappeared. If you want me to say I've screwed things up royally, that I'm a colossal fuckup, then there! I've said it! Is there anything else you'd like from me?"

"Yeah," Les said. "I'd like for you to chill out, for one thing. But there's something else too."

When she looked up into the mirror again, her eyes locked with Les's. "You're not going to leave me alone, are you?" Then she sighed. "Okay. What do you want me to do?"

"Go with me to the house. Give me a picture of her to put out on the wire. I won't leave until you do it. You'll be stuck with me the whole damned day."

The clock over the bar read ten-thirty in the morning. Slowly Robin pulled a wad of bills out of

166

her pocket and threw them in the direction of the bartender. Then she turned to face the detective.

"You mean it, don't you, ol' buddy? Sometimes, you're a real pain in the ass, Les. But if it'll make you happy, let's go."

* * * * *

Megan knew Les Knight's unmarked car. She'd seen it numerous times when he'd been out to investigate the phone calls and the messages. This morning she'd seen the car coming down the street in time to duck behind a thick magnolia tree. It had been raining a slow drizzle all morning, and by the time Les pulled away from the house, she was soaked to her underwear.

Nightmarish visions pushed into her mind. Vivid memories that made her legs turn to jelly. And the voices were back. She shook her head as she entered the living room, trying to banish the images and sounds. And for a moment they were gone.

She felt better. What she needed was a change of clothes. She washed her face and combed her hair, then shucked on a dry pair of jeans and a sweatshirt. She felt cold to the core. And her back hurt.

A secret voice somewhere in her gut whispered that she might have to move fast, so she stepped into her Nike Airs and tied them tight. The police were after her for something. She knew it, but no matter how hard she tried to concentrate, she could not remember why.

And her body would not stop shaking. Maybe she needed food. She hadn't eaten for a while. But in the kitchen, sitting on the refrigerator was the mocking head of death. She blinked hard. It changed into the grinning face of her stepfather, then another face, and then another that melted like a spent candle, unrecognizable. Some part of her knew she was only imagining the faces, but another part of her let out a mind-wrenching scream.

She had to kill it. Kill the head. Make it leave her alone. The knife in the sink would do it. Slowly, she reached out and took the knife in her hand. Stay calm. Just stay calm. It can't hurt you, something deep inside her whispered. It was a sentence someone had told her to say to herself once. Who had said that? She couldn't remember. But it worked when she said it. The head disappeared.

The clock over the stove ticked away time. She was standing in the dining room, staring at the blood, the blood that was dripping from the table onto the carpet. It was coming through the ceiling, running down the wall in thin rivulets. She even smelled the cloying, coppery smell. Running and dripping. Running and dripping.

She held out her hand to catch the gory drops, then looked at her palm. There was nothing there. Suddenly she hooked her fingers, made a claw and raked it across her own cheek, bringing blood, but feeling nothing. With her palm, she spread blood on her face, down her chin and on her forehead. She smeared some on the wall before she licked it from her long fingers, one after another. Then she whined a low whine. Her green eyes glittered, feverish.

BLOOD. BAD. KILL. MURDER. The words

caromed in her skull and took her breath away. Where were the words coming from?

She had to get away from the voice. She reeled into the living room, holding the knife loosely in her hand, and headed for the front door.

Down the front steps and into the street she ran headlong without conscious thought or plan.

She would get them all. All the faces. All the voices. All the tormenters of her soul. She would kill them every one. And she would do it now.

* * * * *

By the time the sky finally cleared, it was late afternoon. After French had gone, Dexter Spencer sat at the table before the window overlooking the lake. He was no fool. He could see that French was right. Things were about to fall down around their ears. The death of the girl made the old plan too risky. Sure, he could report her missing, claiming she was a runaway, but that wouldn't help the authorities from picking and poking around Enlightenment. They'd at least discover the excavating that had already been done and ask questions about that. And he was not at all sure that Munsington would keep his mouth shut. Under pressure, the man just might blab about everything.

One more test. And if that went well, he knew what he must do next. One more test for Roger Plank. He might as well get on with it. He unlocked the door of the next room and called to the two men waiting there.

The first man to emerge was Plank. Mild-mannered Roger Plank, vice-president of the First Commonwealth Bank. He was about five-feet-eight with pale hazel eyes, and wearing a robe. His sandy hair was combed back neatly. He was in his late thirties or early forties and, in spite of his wiry build, he was as strong as an ox. His hobby was weight-lifting.

Close on his heels was Odell Munsington. His eyes looked slightly glazed. Earlier in the afternoon, Spencer had forced him to drink coffee laced with the white powder from his own plastic bag. Forced him at gunpoint.

"Stop there," Spencer said, pointing to a spot on the floor. "You will do what I tell you to."

"Of course, Mr. Spencer," Plank said.

"You too, Odell."

Munsington's mouth turned down at the corners. He was struggling inside.

"Odell!"

"Yes."

"You will obey me and you will be happy about it! Now smile."

"Yes." He smiled as he was told.

"What is about to happen here is for the best. I want you both to understand that. It is for everybody's good in the long run."

"For everybody's good," Plank parroted. He grinned happily.

"We must move quickly. You are to follow me into the woods by the lake. And you will do as you are told. Understood?"

"Understood," Plank said.

"Odell?"

"Understood."

Within fifteen minutes they came to an open spot in the woods. Spencer dropped the canvas bag he was carrying.

"There are shovels and picks in that bag," he told the two men. "Pick them up and begin digging. I want each of you to dig a deep hole, as big as a grave. Now start."

Once again, Munsington looked distressed.

"Relax, Odell. You'll be just fine. This is for everybody's good. It's for the best."

"Relax. It's for the best." Odell seemed to be instructing himself instead of echoing Spencer's words.

The men dug like a pair of cemetery workmen until Spencer told them to stop. There were two holes, each about eight feet deep and three feet across.

"Go behind those trees over there, Odell. You'll find Maxie's body covered with a piece of canvas. Get it and drop it into the hole." Spencer watched him closely for any sign of rebellion. The drug had not had long to do its work. But Munsington did as he was told.

"Now cover her up," Spencer said.

Munsington sweated heavily as he shoveled the dirt. Then suddenly his movements were arrested by a spell of uncontrolled shivering. His thick stomach twisted, and he was short of breath. His jowly face turned slightly purple.

For a moment, Spencer thought he might go into a seizure, but then he was calm again. "Finish the job, Odell," Spencer barked.

Munsington followed his orders, filling the hole and tamping it smooth.

At Spencer's signal, Plank sprinted silently to the edge of the woods and returned dragging scraggly pine and maple branches. He placed them haphazardly over the grave.

Taking his gun from his hip pocket, Spencer said, "Now, Roger, I want you to point this gun at Odell. Odell, I want you to stand perfectly still. Roger is going to shoot you and you are going to let him. This is for everybody's good. Understood?"

"Understood," Roger said, still grinning.

Munsington's mouth turned down at the corners again, but he did not move.

"Pull the trigger, Roger."

Munsington shook his head once, then stopped. Spencer could see muscles in his face and neck bunch up. His arms grew tense and his face flushed.

"Pull the trigger," Spencer told Plank. "Now!"

The gun barked. Munsington fell backward. A slight stench floated on the air as his bladder and bowels turned loose. Roger had hit him square in the heart.

"Give me the gun, Roger. How do you feel?"

"I feel wonderful."

"Tired?"

"Of course not!"

Together they dragged Odell to the open grave and dropped him in. Then they covered him with dirt.

"It's for the best, don't you think?" Spencer said to Plank when they had finished spreading branches over the place.

"Oh, yes! It's the thing to do all right. It's for everybody's good."

His smile was sweet and his eyes sparkled. He looked at Spencer with something that might have been love.

CHAPTER TWELVE

The Atlas Chemicals production plant and offices were located just off Interstate 64 in the heart of Richmond. The building was white brick with green trim. The grounds were neat as a new haircut.

Billie's FBI identification had gotten her past Worth French's secretary with a minimum of to-do. Not that she had anticipated a problem. She knew drug companies lived in holy horror of government censorship and rolled out the red carpet for anyone from any government branch.

French's office was near the front of the plant. It

had a large bay window that overlooked the manicured lawn. In the center of the acre of Kentucky bluegrass was a small fountain with a vertical flume in the middle. Crystal clear water spurted upward, then fell down again, forming never-ending circles on the pool's surface.

French stared out the window at the pool as he said, "We keep twenty or so rare types of goldfish in that pond. It's a little silly really. The maintenance men feed them and clean the fountain, but they're the only people who ever see the expensive little freeloaders. None of the walkways pass by the fountain, and the offices are too far away for anybody to see them. We put the fish in originally because that was part of the architect's plan. People get on a track, don't they? Then don't know when to quit." He had been talking incessantly since Billie entered the room. A long soliloquy on the virtues of Mr. Coffee machines versus other brands had followed his pouring each of them a cup of coffee.

Billie looked at the man's back with a certain amount of pity. In some ways, he was as much a victim of Dexter Spencer as the Cutters were. Spencer had found all their weaknesses and sucked them dry, like a spider draws the life blood from a fly.

Just now, both Billie and French knew they were delaying the inevitable. Was what she was about to do to the man any less ruthless than what others had done to him? She thought it probably wasn't, and felt strangely sorry for him.

It was a quarter past three. "Mr. French," she said gently. "There's no use putting this off any longer. With the cooperation of the IRS, I have ordered an audit of your personal finances and the ACI books. It's already underway. It should be finished by early tomorrow. But I think we both know what they'll find, don't we?"

She was bluffing. The auditing of a company as large as ACI might take a week or two but she needed some answers from him. Now.

French turned, fingered the business card she had given him, and stared solemnly at it for a full minute. As if he had reached some awful decision deep in his soul, he sat down abruptly behind his desk and steepled his fingers.

"I'll tell you something, Agent Robinson. I'm not sure how my life got into the mess it's in. For the past twenty years, it's been like I've been riding a runaway train. One horrible mistake has led to another. Now the Dexter Spencer thing —" His voice trailed off. He seemed to shrink into a small, frail man with an unhealthy yellow complexion.

"You could be accused of being an accomplice to murder, you know." Billie slipped her shoes off underneath the man's desk and unobtrusively massaged one foot with the other.

"Yes," French said, not bothering to wonder how she knew about that. "That's all I've thought about all day."

Billie could sense that he was ready for a confession, that he would feel relieved to finally tell the truth and be done with it, no matter what the consequences. She decided to play on that vulnerability.

"Listen carefully, Mr. French. I have a proposal to offer you. The FBI is not terribly interested in the fact that you've taken a little money from the company till. After all, it is your company. You built it. You run it. The IRS will care about that, of course, but I can urge them to allow you to make amends without filing criminal charges against you."

French's sharp intake of breath filled the room. Some small amount of color came back into his face.

"In fact," Billie went on, "I might, just might, be able to help get the syndicate off your back. You may be aware of the fact that the FBI and those slimeballs do a little mutual back scratching when it becomes the expedient thing to do."

French tried hard to control his breathing but his chest rose and fell a little faster in response to her words. For the first time since she entered his office, there was a tiny bit of hope in his eyes. "I've heard rumors. What would I have to do?"

"Not much, really. I just want you to tell me what's going on at Enlightenment. I want you to tell me everything you know and even what you think you might know. I especially want to hear about what Roger Plank's role is in all this. Will you tell me? Tell me the truth?"

He sat back in his chair and seemed to visibly relax. His breath came more quietly. "At this point, Agent Robinson, I don't see that I have any other choice, so you can be sure that anything I tell you is the absolute truth. If you can help me with the syndicate — The truth there is that if I don't come up with the money I owe them within a month, I'm almost certainly a dead man anyway."

"All I can promise is to try. But I will promise that."

French pressed the intercom button. "Hold all my calls, Rachel," he said to his secretary.

"Yes sir."

"On second thought," he said. "You might as well go on home, Rachel. This is going to take the rest of the day. No use waiting around for me. I'll close up the office."

"Thank you, sir. Thank you very much." She sounded touched. She liked French. He had always been good to her.

He sat back in his chair, joined his hands in front of him. "Now where shall I begin?" he began.

* * * * *

Neglected paperwork had kept Stephanie at the office later than she had planned. She had gotten woefully behind on her case notes, and it was nearly time for her quarterly meeting with her accountant.

When she did get home, the house was dark. The mercury-vapor lamp on the street corner cast a frieze of elongated shadows across the lawn, and where the light fell, the grass looked more purple than green.

The engine of her Cutlass hissed softly as she walked from the driveway to the house. Idly, she wondered if something was wrong with it. The car was nearly new, but she hadn't taken the time to have all the warranty service inspections done. Too busy. Too many complications in her life. Maybe she'd get around to it tomorrow. Always tomorrow.

The night air was cool but heavy, as if the morning rain water still saturated it. The smell of rotting mulch rose up to greet her as she passed neglected flowerbeds. Perhaps she would weed them this weekend.

She slipped the key into the lock, opened the

door and flipped on the hallway light. The house seemed dank and stale.

Without turning on more lights, she walked to the den and raised a window. A noise behind her, like shuffling feet, caused her to turn. Fear filled her throat and her heart thumped painfully in her chest.

In the light from the street, she could see the dim outline of a woman's body. Cautiously, she reached for the floor lamp switch and flooded the room. The brightness momentarily blinded her.

When her pupils adjusted, she recognized the woman. "Megan?" she said uneasily. "How did you get in?"

"Not Megan. Beth. I'm Beth. Robin has a key. I took it." The woman moved toward her, then stopped about six feet away. A broad grin spread across her face and she licked lightly at her lips.

Stephanie started as she saw the blood smeared grotesquely on her chin and across her forehead like war paint.

"What do you want, Megan? What are you doing here?"

"Want to see you, bitch! Settle our differences." The voice was Megan's voice, only deeper and more full of venom. The green eyes were glassy and yellow, like a cat's just before it seizes a bird in its jaws. Her hair hung like strands of dirty hemp.

"We have no differences, Megan." Stephanie backed away.

"Beth, you bitch! I'm Beth!" She took a step forward. "Been waiting here for you all day. You've messed up Megan's life all you're going to."

"You're scaring me, Megan. I mean, Beth. Don't do this. I'd like you to leave now."

Another step. Then another in Stephanie's direction. Slowly. Carefully. "Megan is a milquetoast. I'm the one who has to take care of that little shit. All she knows how to do is whimper and yell her stupid head off. I know she threatened you. I heard her. But she really wouldn't do anything. I'm the one who knows what to do to take care of things." She laughed loudly.

Stephanie had backed up against her writing desk. Briefly she considered searching behind her for a weapon. A letter opener. A paperweight. Anything. Then she thought better of it. There was no way she could do physical harm to this woman. This woman who was now so obviously insane. It was true she had managed to hurt Greg Rooney, but this was something different. Entirely different. She slid the desk chair between them.

The world seemed to shift into slow motion. Stephanie watched fascinated as Megan moved toward her, moving like the air had turned into thick syrupy mud. Stephanie's heartbeat felt flighty, jittery. Her breath seemed to have frozen in her lungs as she watched Megan coming. Relentlessly. Grinning. Enjoying the chase. Moving slowly. Megan giggled like a small child.

It was then that Stephanie saw the knife. It crossed her mind that she had read that women rarely commit crimes of violence. And when they do, they almost never use a knife. Maybe it's because to use a knife you have to get in really close. Breathe the air the victim breathes. Smell the fear coming from the pores of the intended. Maybe it's too intimate an experience, so that the killer must be willing to let the blood spatter in her face and on her lips where she can taste it.

Then Megan was on her — so close she could smell her sour sweat. She placed the very tip of the knife carefully at Stephanie's throat. And laughed. Laughed like the Devil himself was in her soul. Laughed like demons screaming with the insane humor of Hades. She moved the knife slowly, deliberately bringing a furrow of blood to the surface of Stephanie's neck. Then, unpredictably, she stuck out her tongue and licked at the blood on the knife.

The sting of the cut brought Stephanie to her senses and snapped her back into real time. She slapped at the knife-wielding hand and scuttled like a crab behind the couch. Her insides felt like gelatin and her knees went rubbery.

With no warning, the fear in her heart gave way to anger. This was *her* space. *Her* house. *Her* body. And crazy or not, this woman was trying to kill her. Then anger gave way to fury.

"Get out of my house!" she screamed. "Get out! Get out of here! Now!"

Megan shook her head left and right, then bared her teeth. "I'll kill you," she said, and her face took on the mask of the stalking animal as she narrowed her eyes to slits and grinned. The vampire's grin. The yellowed dripping fangs of the tiger. She made a fencer's lunge in Stephanie's direction.

With a small cry, Stephanie gripped the sofa hard with both hands and tipped it away from her toward Megan.

Megan jumped back, easily out of the way, as the heavy furniture fell impotently on the floor. She stepped up onto the cushions. The knife was now only a foot or two away from Stephanie's heart.

Stephanie's breath came in ragged gasps as Megan made tiny circles with the knife — and the fury melted into fear again. The door. If she could make it to the door, she could run. Get away. She darted to her left. Megan blocked her path.

"Whore," Megan said between clenched teeth. "I hate women. All whores. You won't get away from me. None of the others did."

"Others? What others?" Maybe she could buy some time. Her heart was hammering furiously, and her stomach felt cold, like she had swallowed some huge block of ice.

Megan came at her again. "I'll cut your goddamned head off." She waved the knife at her, slashing the air as if cutting away at some invisible barrier.

"Megan! Beth! Tell me about the others! Who were they? What did they do to you?"

Megan took another step. "You know them, Lucifer's mother! Satan's daughter! You were in them all." Her cold eyes gleamed feverishly.

In all of her days of working with disturbed patients, Stephanie had never seen such insanity in a person's eyes. The eyes of the mentally ill are usually flat and empty as if they have lost all feeling, all caring. Megan's eyes were glistening, shining eyes, full of passionate desire and wanting. Monstrous eyes. The werewolf's eyes.

Suddenly Stephanie was crying. Tears tracked silently down her cheeks and onto her lips. She licked them and made a small whimpering sound in the back of her throat. She was not weeping out of fear. Or out of anger. Some corner of her consciousness had finally recognized that there was no escape. She was cornered by the predator, like a helpless animal. She shuddered with despair. For the first time in her life, it came to her that she must consider the possibility of seriously harming another human being. Perhaps killing in defense of her own life. The great paradox of all debates of pacifism echoed in her brain. Would you kill to keep from being killed? Or kill to protect a loved one? Now the rhetoric had become reality. She had only moments to make her decision. Then she decided.

"Megan. Or Beth. Whoever you are. I'm going to walk out of here. I'm going to walk by you to the door. I'm going to leave. And you're going to let me." She took a step to her left.

"No!" Megan said. She whipped the knife through the air again. Her eyes glowed, nearly red in their passion.

Stephanie took a tiny step. "Yes, I am. I'm going to walk out of this room and out of this house."

"Like hell!" Megan yelled. Her breath was coming in noisy pants.

Stephanie's own breath was shallow and labored as she moved sideways, inching toward the door. She bumped the side of the fish tank with her hip. "If you have to hurt me, you just will. I won't be able to stop you. But Megan would not want that. She may be angry with me because she thinks I've hurt her, but she would not want you to harm me."

"Megan! Shit! I'll spread your guts all over this room. Megan doesn't know shit. She lets all of them hurt her! She never tells. She never does anything!"

Stephanie heard the bubble of the filter in the

fish tank over the sound of their breathing. She moved again, wishing the gigantic tank sat further from the wall so she could put it between them. If she could just get out of the den and lock the door behind her. She reached far down in soul and got a grip on her panic.

"Megan, I'm going out that door. And when I do, I want you to stay back. Stay away from me. Is that clear?"

Megan glared at her. Then, inexplicably, she dropped her eyes to the fish tank.

"Do you hear me, Megan? It's *you* I'm talking to. Not Beth. You, Megan, must listen to me. You're going to let me leave."

Stephanie drew back as the woman took one more menacing step toward her. Megan blinked. Her eyes seemed to change. They were no longer hard as they had been, but watery. Then suddenly soft as she looked down at the aquarium.

"Can I feed the fish?" she asked in a moment. The voice was a little girl voice. Light and airy. Even friendly.

Stephanie stood stone still.

"Pretty fish!" Megan gushed, childlike. "Can I feed them? Please, lady, can I feed them?"

Stephanie shivered as she watched the transformation of Megan take place. "Who are you, little girl?" she ventured.

"My name is Melody. Can I feed the fish?"

In spite of a feeling of horror, Stephanie realized what was happening. Megan was completely disassociating. Switching personalities like changing dresses. Stephanie had never seen a case of multiple personalities. She was not even sure she believed in such a thing. Not the way it was presented in books and movies, anyway. But standing before her was certainly the personality of a little girl in a grown woman's body.

Stephanie sagged back against the wall, but she did not take her eyes off the knife. Beth could return at any moment. "Give me the knife, Melody, and you can feed the fish." Slowly, she reached for the can of fish food on the top of the tank and held it out in front of her.

"I wanted some fish from the dime store, but she wouldn't buy me any." She held out her hand for the food, but the knife stayed where it was.

Then Stephanie bolted. She was almost down the front steps when she realized that Megan might have faked the whole thing. Might not have really been the little girl person at all. She could have staged the change to draw her close and strike her by surprise. Too late now.

She slammed the car door hard and slapped at the locks. The keys! Where were the keys? On the table in the den!

A moment later she heard the front door slam with a loud *bang*.

Megan was carrying something in her hand. The knife? Perhaps it was the fish food. She watched, her heart lying icy in her chest, as the woman walked slowly down the street and into the darkness. Out of sight.

Stephanie leaned her head against the steering wheel and wept.

CHAPTER THIRTEEN

Billie strained to hear any sound other than her own footsteps. Without benefit of even a flashlight, she had made her way from the hard surface road across the fields of the Enlightenment property until she found a footpath that crossed the woods and came out behind the old chapel.

She had come alone, hoping to find hard evidence against Spencer — papers, logs, journals — anything that would not be disputable in court. Worth French's testimony would help, but given his own indiscretions, his word alone might not be good enough. And she was determined to put Spencer away for good.

The underbrush was soaked with dew and her socks and canvas Reeboks were growing heavier by the minute. Even her jeans were wet up to the knees. Her Smith & Wesson .38 Special was tucked away, high and dry in the shoulder holster, underneath a lightweight navy windbreaker.

It was nearly dawn by the time she reached the commune's main buildings. She arrived just in time to watch from a distance as Dexter Spencer patted a well-dressed Roger Plank on the back and walked him to his car. Plank's three-piece banker's suit fit perfectly with the gray Chrysler New Yorker he climbed into. The engine caught smoothly.

Spencer wore his usual monk's garb. He watched Plank drive away, then turned and walked steadily toward the dining hall. A pair of male cultists dressed in robes and sandals joined him and matched his pace, step for step. Uzi carbines hung by leather straps across their muscled shoulders.

Billie crouched behind a wall of shrubbery until Spencer and his guards disappeared from sight. Then, moving from pine tree to pine tree, she made her way to the office building.

Cautiously, she mounted the steps and tested the door. It was open. She reached under her jacket and drew out the pistol. Holding her breath, she pushed the door wide and stepped forward, swinging the gun in an arc to the left and then to the right.

And came face to face with a totally bald, stoop-shouldered, heavy man with a curly beard. He was dressed in the sandals and robe of a commune member. A look of terror flooded his green eyes as he focused on the gun.

"Don't hurt me," the man said. "Please don't hurt me."

Billie lowered her gun and moved toward him.

"What are you doing here?" she asked him. "You work in Spencer's office?"

He nodded.

"What do you do? What's your job?"

"Filing. Typing. Office work," he stuttered. "Don't hurt me please."

"I'm not going to hurt you," she promised. "Not if you cooperate. Where does Spencer keep his important papers? His books. Tell me!"

He didn't answer, but swallowed and shook his head vigorously.

Billie stood silent for a moment, trying to guess whether the man didn't know or was refusing to tell her.

"Listen to me!" Billie said. "I'm with the FBI. Tell me where he keeps his papers. Where does he hide things?"

The man's eyes grew huge with fear, but he remained mute. His whole frame shook visibly.

Billie felt fleeting guilt about intimidating the quivering little man. He didn't deserve it. Spencer did. But she couldn't afford to waste more time. If she were discovered now, she'd be a dead woman.

She grabbed him roughly by the front of his robe and pulled him to her. "I'm giving you one last chance! For your own good, you'd better tell me! Where are the papers?"

To Billie's surprise, the man smiled sweetly and

relaxed. "Yes," he said. "It's for my own good. It's for everybody's good. Mr. Spencer put papers in the box. It's under the floor in the next room."

Suddenly it struck her. Alice had claimed Mark had said those very words to her — that Spencer had told him what he was doing was for his own good, everybody's good. It made sense now. The people — the important people anyway — were given the lodestar, then programmed to respond only to a request that was followed by "it's for your own good." That way, Spencer, and only Spencer, could control their behavior. The girl, Maxie, must not have been important enough to get Spencer's full programming package or she wouldn't have responded to Munsington's commands. Billie felt sad at the irony of it. Maxie's lack of importance had caused her death.

"Show it to me," she said.

It was a metal strong box with a hasp and no lock tucked under a two-foot square of removable boards.

"What the shit?" she said as she opened the box to find a stash of plastic bags tightly packed with a grayish powder.

"Lodestar," she whispered.

At the bottom of the box, there were two large manila envelopes. She opened the first one, whistled when she saw the contents, and slipped it inside her jacket. The second one contained names and addresses. People of the commune? She quickly searched for Mark Cutter's name, found it, and saw the figure, two-hundred-thousand dollars, beside it. There was also a penciled note: *more available from his mother.*

189

She thought of searching the rest of the building, then heard voices. She moved swiftly to the door leading outside and opened it enough to see through. Commune members were streaming from the dining hall. Spencer and his henchmen were unsettlingly close and moving fast through the woods in her direction.

Billie looked the building over quickly, but there was no door leading outside which she could leave by without being seen.

The green-eyed man stood by watching, but making no attempt to interfere. Billie turned to him. "What's you name," she demanded. "It's for your own good that you tell me."

"Malcolm Conrad."

"Well, Malcolm. I'm awfully sorry to have to do this to you, but I need your clothes. Give me your robe."

"But I —"

"Give it to me," she said. "For your own good."

Obediently, the man stripped down to his underwear.

* * * * *

Megan had walked for hours trying to find her own neighborhood. As the sun came up, she finally hailed a cab, convinced the driver that her boyfriend had roughed her up, then dumped her in a strange part of town. She got him to agree to take her home with the promise of a fifty-dollar tip when they got there. He waited while she went inside and found the money to pay him.

When she had washed her face and changed her

clothes, she stared bleakly at herself in the mirror and wondered if this was a new phase of her somnambulism. She hadn't gone wandering about the streets in years. In fact she had not left the house like that since . . . Megan shook her head. Who was Evelyn?

Ralph and her mother had been drinking all day. She had begged to go to the skating rink, but Ralph had said no even though she had finished her chores. Mama always made her do whatever Ralph said, and he said he wanted her around to bring him cold beer. In the afternoon, Ralph and Mama had gone into the bedroom and Evelyn had heard them argue loudly, then moan softly, while bedsprings squeaked.

Evelyn sat on the vanity bench in front of the mirror and combed her hair, trying out one colorful ribbon after another. She sang to herself, trying to block out the unpleasant sounds from the other end of the house, as she appraised her ten-year-old body. She thought her face was too thin and she had too many freckles, but people always said she was pretty.

Ralph said so too. But she wished he didn't think so.

She jumped when she saw Ralph's naked body appear at her doorway. She hadn't heard him coming.

"Your mama's asleep," he said. He came over to her and kissed the top of her head.

"Guess you want me to get you another beer." *Evelyn said and stood up, trying to escape his stinking breath and the embarrassing sight of his nakedness.*

He grabbed her shoulders and pushed her back

down. Hard. "I want a real kiss first. Kiss Daddy, pretty baby," he said. And cupped a dirty hand under each of her budding breasts. He grinned at her in the mirror and licked his swollen lips.

"You ain't my daddy," she said.

"I know that," he said. "That's why you like me to do this." He shoved his hand under her bottom and lifted her onto the bed behind him. He was kissing her hard and he had his hand between her legs. She fought like a wild person when he tried to move her hand to his crotch.

"Ralph?"

She heard her mother's voice. Then the sound of her feet padding across the floor. She heard her mother's loud cough as she came to the door of the bedroom.

"Oh, shit," her mother said.

Then Evelyn heard her shuffle on to the kitchen and heard the refrigerator door open.

It was when the top of the beer can popped that she swore to herself she would kill Ralph the first chance she got and maybe her mother too.

All she remembered now was that they had found her wandering the streets in a daze a few days later.

But she put even that out of her head as she crawled between the clean sheets. She was tired. She would be able to think more clearly when she had had some rest.

* * * * *

Billie had expected Spencer to come immediately into the office building. Instead, he stopped in front and waited while the twenty-five or thirty people from the dining hall gathered around him.

He made a sweeping motion with his hand and the crowd dropped into sitting positions on the ground. The armed henchmen stood behind him, guns lowered.

After placing a square of red velvet on the ground in front of him, Spencer closed his eyes and meditated briefly. His followers waited silently until he opened his eyes and spoke.

"We shall begin the sacrifice! Barbara Newton! Come here!" he thundered.

A woman rose and approached him. She was fiftyish and dark, with a hint of a mustache across her upper lip. She lowered her eyes shyly, then dropped awkwardly to her knees in front of him.

"Barbara, what gifts have you brought the master today?" Spencer asked, touching her hair lightly.

Spencer rocked back on his heels and smiled with pleasure as she emptied her pockets. There was a handful of jewelry. Strings of pearls, rings, bracelets of rubies and diamonds and other assorted gems spilled out on the red velvet.

She giggled and moved back to her place on the ground.

"Amos Hall," Spencer called.

A black man with an Afro and a graying beard stood and came forward. He too dropped to his knees.

"And what do you bring, Amos?"

"Money," Amos said. "As you asked."

The next person was a woman named Flora Pinkney. And she was followed by a skinny little man named Graham Lee who looked anemic.

In the course of fifteen minutes, as Billie watched from the window not thirty feet away, twenty more of Spencer's flock lay valuables at his feet.

The two sentries had set their guns on the ground and were leaning against a tree looking bored. Spencer motioned to them and they came forward to gather up the gifts.

Spencer spoke to the crowd. "You have all done well this week. As we know, this is for the good of Enlightenment and for your own good as well. God will bless you for your good works."

A murmur of agreement arose from the members.

Spencer went on. "You know your future assignments. You are to continue to give what you own. Your homes, businesses, your savings must all be given to Enlightenment. For your own good."

"Yes," the people said as one.

"And when that is done, you must find other ways to give. Use your credit cards. Get bank loans. Talk to those who love you. Persuade them of your need. Steal only if you have to. We must not lose good people like yourselves."

Billie had seen and heard enough.

She stepped through the front door and made her way toward Spencer. The robe she had taken from Malcolm Conrad hid her clothes and her gun nicely. She drew the hood up over her hair and kept her head down as she walked. Spencer appeared not to notice her until she stood almost in front of him.

Without preamble, she said to him, "Still up to your old tricks, are you, Spencer? Or should I call you Smythe? Or maybe you prefer Spilka?"

"What the fuck?" he said as she pulled back her hood. "Why, you're that damned patrolman. What the hell are you doing here? And in that getup."

"Cut the crap, Spencer. I know all about you. Who you are and who you have been." She pulled back her sleeve to let him catch a glimpse of the gun she held in her hand.

He backed away from her. His right hand went to his cheek and stroked his beard. "Do you have business here? Have you come to join the commune?" he said, apparently unruffled.

"Knock it off," Billie said. "I know all about what's been going on here. Everything. I saw what just went on here. I even know about the murder."

"My dear lady, whoever you may be, you are speaking nonsense. There's been no *murder* here."

"I suppose you don't know anything about these either." Billie reached under her robe and pulled out the envelope. She dumped an inch-thick stack of Polaroid pictures on the ground.

For a moment he just stared at the photos, then he picked them up and flipped through them, one by one. "Where did you get these? Who are you? You're obviously not just some highway patrolman."

"Not exactly. Now let's talk business."

He stared at her, his gaze so intense it was

almost tangible. Billie found it hard not to look away from his black eyes. "How about the business of trespassing on my land?" he said.

"How about two-hundred-thousand dollars worth of business?"

"Are you trying to sell me these pictures? Is this some kind of blackmail?" His tone mocked her.

"The two hundred thousand is the money you owe Mark Cutter. And that's just a drop in the bucket compared to the millions you've bilked people out of with all your scams. Blackmail is your favorite game though, isn't it? Or it was until you happened upon this place. How did you find out about the chemicals in the lake? You couldn't have known about that when you bought this place. My guess is you planned more blackmail and just got lucky with the lake business."

Spencer tried to keep his composure, but he was pulling unconsciously at his beard, rolling the hair between his thumb and forefinger. His mouth had become a hard line. There was no way she could know about the lake chemicals.

"Accusations are worthless, dear lady. If you have any proof that I have . . . done anything illegal . . . then show me. All you've seen here this morning are generous people giving generous gifts to Enlightenment."

"Let me see now," Billie began. "What proof do I have? How about Roger Plank's testimony that you coerced him, under the influence of drugs of course, into bank robbery? Not enough?"

Spencer laughed. He had programmed Roger to say it was all his idea to take the money from the bank if he were caught. She was bluffing.

"I'd say I don't know what you're talking about."

"And if Worth French testifies for the prosecution? Will that be enough? What if he tells how you've drugged the people here to get them to do whatever you've wanted? Think that'll be enough?"

Momentarily, he looked a little stunned. Then he laughed out loud. "Sleazy little coward, French. Let him testify. I'll say it was all his idea. That I didn't know anything about any of it. He's been stealing from his own company. No doubt you know about that too. Who the shit's going to believe him?"

"And what about these pictures? They *are* pictures of you, aren't they? You, accepting money from Senator Houser? And from Congressman Tatum? What did you do, Spencer? You take porno pictures of them doing it with some aide? Or did you catch them sniffing up snow with a straw? I'm afraid I didn't take the time to find out the exact details of all your little games in Washington. But I know about them."

Spencer didn't miss a beat. "Or maybe I did some work for those men they were paying me for. Those pictures aren't worth a goddamned thing."

"But they are, my slimy friend. I think Houser and Tatum will finally agree to testify against you — after I tell them about the trick you've tried to pull here at Enlightenment. Even fear of exposure of whatever you have on them isn't enough for them to let you threaten our national security. French told me you planned to sell this chemical of yours to a foreign country."

Spencer stared off into space and looked thoughtful. Then he whistled softly between his teeth. As if he were calling a dog. "Washington's full of shitty little assholes," he said, his voice heavy with disdain. "Screwing around. Doing dope of every description. Bunch of jewboys and niggers. Faggots, too. Then they sit back with their cushy little jobs and act as holy as Jesus Christ himself. Nasty slime pots! They deserve everything they get. And you're right. I've gotten a few of them in my day. Call it a public service. Tatum and Houser won't testify. They'd have to give up their sweet little pockets of power to do that. They'd have to admit to all their little indiscretions. Besides, dear lady, you'll never live to turn me in."

They were suddenly surrounded by people the from the commune. Spencer gestured for them to move closer. He stepped back out of the ring they formed.

"It's no wonder that Washington's finest want to hang onto their jobs, is it?" Spencer said, with a broad smirk. "It's wonderful to have people at your beck and call. Just a whistle and here they are. I've learned to enjoy it."

"Get them out of here, Spencer. These people are not to blame for your evil. They haven't done anything wrong." Billie raised her Smith & Wesson then lowered it, knowing she wouldn't use it against innocent people.

"Do you also know, smart lady, that they'll do anything I tell them to do? Even kill?"

"You're making a big mistake, Spencer. Don't do this!"

"Peter! Steve!" he barked at his guards. "Take her to the pond and fill her full of the lake water. Make her drink it till she vomits."

Two large men stepped forward and took Billie's arms. Their eyes were blank. Their faces empty of any emotion. Spencer gave another signal and they lifted her off the ground, suspended between them. They dragged her in the direction of the lake.

CHAPTER FOURTEEN

Robin Oakley poured her second cup of coffee from the big urn at the police station. She looked at it in revulsion. There had been too much of the acidic liquid going down her throat since Megan had run away from the hospital. Les Knight had seen to that.

She put her hands over her eyes and clutched her temples. She was getting a headache. Probably a delayed hangover. Her stomach felt like a garbage can.

Les had sent a picture of Megan out over the fax machine the day before, sent it to every state, every city in the entire country. Now he was fussing around the office, finding one stupid chore after another to keep himself — and her — busy.

Robin sat at her desk, gazing disgustedly at the pile of paperwork he had dumped on her. She knew what he was up to. Anything to keep her out of the squad car and off patrol. Every muscle in her body ached to be out there searching the streets for Megan, but Les would have none of it. She felt so helpless, just sitting at the station.

Les strolled in the vicinity of her desk. "How're you doing?"

"I've got a pain in my ass," she came back. "And it's name is Les Knight."

He shrugged. "Hardly an original name. Why don't you call it Blue? Blue Knight! Now there's a name befitting a policewoman's pain in the ass! Get it? Blue Knight? Cops dressed in blue?"

Robin almost laughed. Les was a sweet guy. And she knew he only had her best interests at heart. He had helped her along since she was a rookie cop. Had been a kind of mentor, one minority to another, when none of the white males had shown the inclination. And the two of them shared another bond. Each believed deeply in the good of the career they had chosen. Believed with a passion that approached fanaticism in society's need for law and order.

Robin kept her face rigid. She knew him well. The jokes were what he used to set the stage for bad news. "I'm not stupid, Les. I get it. What's up your sleeve?"

Les pulled up a chair. "Listen, Robin, I have some new information. I just got a call from Stephanie Scott. Megan paid her a visit last night. Said she was acting like her brains were scrambled."

"Last night? And she *just* called you?"

She stared at him with disbelief. "Seems Stephanie couldn't get to a phone. Megan was waiting for her when she got home from work. Threatened her with a knife. She got away from her somehow and locked herself in the car. She was afraid to come out until daylight." He kept his voice level, not wanting to frighten her with the details.

Robin swallowed hard. "Is she all right? Stephanie, I mean?"

"She's just fine, but from what she told me, Megan's not. I don't know much of that psychology doubletalk, but you remember that movie called *Sybil*? Stephanie thinks it's something like that. More than one personality. The technical name for it is *dissociative reaction*. I think that's what she said."

"Jesus Christ, we have to find Megan!"

"We do," Les agreed. "I've got all the patrol cars looking for her. That's all we can do. But there's something else, Robin."

The tone of his voice frightened her. "Tell me, Les. Out with it."

"I just got a message over the wire. Megan's name is really Evelyn Hightower. She's from Waco, Texas, originally. She escaped from a Texas prison for the criminally insane about seven months ago. Seems her father had left her money and she cleaned out the bank accounts before she left the state. Don't know exactly how she managed that, but she did."

Robin didn't want to ask the next question, but she had to know. "What was she in prison for?"

Les rubbed his hand over his mouth. He didn't want to tell her, but he had to. "She killed her mother and stepfather. There's some speculation that the stepfather raped her. Maybe had sexually abused her for years. Possibly her mother didn't try to stop him. She hasn't been in any shape to tell anybody what really happened. Whatever it was sent her right over the edge."

"My God! Am I an idiotic ass, Les? Why didn't I know something was wrong?"

"Stephanie said you'd say that. She said to tell you there was no way you could have known. The Megan personality — that part of her — has been dominant during the time she's been here with you and was normal enough. Stephanie said to tell you she didn't see what was happening either and she's trained to see such things."

Robin stood up. She was trembling from head to toe.

"Are you okay?" he asked.

"No," she said. "No, I'm not. What if we don't catch her, Les?"

"I told you we would."

"I know what you said. But she got away from that prison in Texas. I have to get out of here, Les. Jesus! I have to go."

She pushed past him before he could stop her.

* * * * *

The others stepped aside to let Peter and Steve pass, then closed ranks behind them. Billie Robinson fought them with all of her strength, but the two of them were too much. They took her gun and pitched it aside. Then each one took an arm and lifted her off the ground.

Dexter Spencer had not moved from the spot where he stood, but he couldn't pass up one parting shot. "Now we'll see who's the smart one, won't we?" he yelled after the crowd. "It won't hurt a bit to have you working for me inside the government. Not one goddamned bit!"

He laughed a horrible laugh. He would have said more, but his rantings were interrupted.

The whirring blades of a helicopter laid a background for the sound of an electronic bullhorn. The noise split the air like summer thunder.

"This is Agent King of the Federal Bureau of Investigation. Release the woman. You are directed to respond immediately. You are surrounded. Do as I say and no one will be hurt."

The people who had been progressing toward the lake with Billie in tow stopped still.

"What in the name of shit!" Spencer exclaimed. He began running toward the main building looking up at the sky as if the eagles had swooped down for their lunch. His shoe caught a tree root and sent him sprawling chin first into the ground.

A second helicopter dipped low, rustling the trees and causing pine cones to rain down on his head. The noise was deafening. Spencer rolled over on his back, spitting dirt, shielding his face with his arm.

The others from the commune stood cemented in place, their mouths open and slack with wonder.

Billie screamed at them, "Let me go! For your own good!"

Then she broke free. No one followed her. She ran for her gun.

From the wooded perimeter, fifteen or twenty men and half a dozen women emerged. They wore flak-jackets over their clothes and carried automatic weapons. Smoothly, they moved to surround the people of the commune, who offered no resistance.

In the background, over the noise of the choppers, Billie could hear the screaming of sirens. She had ordered ambulances to follow as close behind the armed agents as safety would permit. It was crucial to get people to the hospital as quickly as possible.

She stood over Spencer with the Smith & Wesson. "Turn over, jackass, and put your hands behind your back."

He did as he was told. She frisked him thoroughly, slapped handcuffs on his wrists, then rolled him over roughly. No one else had moved near enough to them to hear.

"You knew they were coming?" he asked.

Billie placed the gun barrel at the base of his bobbing Adam's apple. "Would it surprise you to know I've had your office building bugged for weeks? They've been waiting. I merely told them when to come. Now I want to know where the money is hidden."

Spencer glared up at her. "Why should I tell you anything? You won't hurt me. Those agents won't let you."

"Those agents work for me, you piece of shit! Every one of them will testify that you tried to kill me and I had to shoot you in order to defend myself. Now tell me where you have the money hidden."

Spencer's mouth worked frantically, but no sound came out. He shook his head.

"How would you like to have a piece of your own medicine then? I just happen to have some of that crap you've been feeding these people. In fact, I have a pocketful. You know it's lethal, don't you? You buried the girl Odell Munsington killed with it, then murdered him. Oh, you had poor Roger pull the trigger, but you murdered him just the same."

Spencer's eyes bulged nearly out of his head.

"Worth French told me. And Roger Plank will back him up. Plank's safely in the hospital, by the way. Now where's the fucking money?" Billie pulled a handful of the gray powder out of her jacket pocket and held it over Spencer's mouth.

He hesitated only a moment longer, then the words poured out of him in a rush. "Don't make me take that stuff. Some of the money's in a safe under the floor of my cabin. There's more in an account in Canada. And there are other accounts. I . . . I didn't want French to know I had it. I thought he'd eventually come up with the money from his company if Plank didn't get it from the bank. You can have it all. Let me go. I'll tell you where it is."

Billie stepped back and looked the man up and down. "A fucking schemer to the end! Thanks, but no thanks. You'll tell me. Or I can always give you a little lodestar cocktail and make you lead me to it."

She walked away. As she passed by the helicopter, she threw a little salute in the direction of Phil King who was loading a group of the Enlightenment people.

"Want a ride?" he called to her.

"I think I'll walk back. I left my car on the road. A hike through the countryside will do my soul good after being this close to the Devil."

CHAPTER FIFTEEN

In the middle of her own bedroom, Robin stood
looking down on the sleeping figure of the woman
Les had said was really Evelyn Hightower. She was
sleeping peacefully, breathing easily. Robin could
barely detect the rise and fall of the thin chest and
breasts of this stranger in the house. She had never
really known her at all.

She wondered when she herself had last gotten a
good night's sleep. And when she might sleep

soundly again. It didn't matter. She was perfectly capable of wandering into nightmares wide awake.

She glanced at her watch. Almost six-thirty. She had driven and walked the streets of Richmond looking for Megan before she came home. There were blisters on both her heels. And the leg with the barely healed wound ached deeply.

Robin crossed the room, stood indecisively by the phone for a moment, then moved to the bedroom door. Better to let her rest. A phone call to Les might wake her. She'd call him from the den phone. God only knew what faced this woman next. At the least, she would be taken back to the Texas prison or insane asylum.

She hesitated as she pulled the door closed. Should she lock it behind her? Megan — rather Evelyn — was no match for her awake, much less half asleep. Vague thoughts about what might happen if she were to awaken passed through her mind, but she dismissed them. Silly to imagine the woman was dangerous. She had lived in the same house with her for months.

She rounded the corner in the hall and started down the steps. The clock in the foyer struck the half hour, then was still. She looked over her shoulder to convince herself that no one was behind her.

She opened the kitchen door for Oodles to go out. The dog ran out barking, then settled down to investigate the fenced yard for new smells. Robin watched a moment, then headed for the den.

Even though the sun had not yet set, the den

seemed dark. Robin took off the heavy uniform jacket, loosened her tie and switched on the lamp by the phone. Maybe a quick drink before she called Les would ease the queasiness in her stomach. She splashed an inch of bourbon into a tumbler.

As she raised the glass to her lips, it came to her that she was not alone. The hair on her arms stood up stiffly. Icy feet climbed up her back.

When she turned, Megan was moving toward her.

At first she wasn't sure it was Megan. The woman's face was familiar, but the eyes were aflame with a murderous red glow; her mouth was slack and a stream of saliva oozed down her chin. The blonde hair was stringy, dirty. She had a hammer in her hand.

"I told you to make him stop, didn't I, Mother, and you wouldn't do it," she whispered. She swung the hammer wildly, making it whistle as it cut the air.

Robin backed away from her, nearly tripping over a footstool. "I'm not your mother, Megan. I mean Evelyn. I'm Robin, remember? Robin Oakley."

"Bitch! You gave me to him to keep him off of you!" Her voice was little more than a hiss.

The hammer came down with a thud on the end table, making a half-dollar sized circle. She swung again quickly, this time catching the lamp. It exploded into a thousand tiny pieces.

It came to Robin in a mind-bending jolt of reality that this woman intended to kill her, meant to beat her to death with the hammer if she could.

"Whore! Bitch!" Megan screamed at her. "You're going to finally get what you deserve. Yes, you will!

I thought I had killed you before. I'll kill you now, by God. You can't get away from me again."

Robin looked for a way to get past her. She would have to vault the sofa. Could she do it fast enough? She had to try or be pinned to the wall.

She began the leap. The hammer caught her in mid-air and buried itself in the soft cushion of her breasts. She fell backward across the coffee table, clutching her chest. The ribs felt broken. She rolled to her left and up on her knees. That was when she saw the kitchen knife. It glittered in Megan's hand.

Knees bent, Robin inched sideways toward the fireplace. Toward the stand of fire tools. Megan anticipated the move and cut her off. Holding her away with the knife, she seized the fire poker.

"No, you won't hurt me any more!" Megan said, grinning. "You can't get away from me this time. Why do you keep coming back anyway, you stinking bitch? What does it take to kill you?" She brought the poker down with all her strength.

Robin's right shoulder seemed to burst apart, exploding in pain. The arm dangled uselessly from her shirt sleeve. She bit her lip hard to stop a cry from escaping her lips. An outburst might excite Megan even more. Blood bubbled down her chin.

The poker whistled toward her head. Instinctively, she ducked and heard the iron rod scream within a hair of her ear. She struggled to her feet. She had to defend herself. Molten terror spread through her insides. Then a blackness like midnight threatened to fill her brain. If she passed out, she was a dead woman. Megan would surely finish her off. Even now she was moving slowly toward her with the weapon pulled back with both hands, up over her head.

Robin kicked with all the strength she could muster into the pit of Megan's stomach. The effort sent spasms of pain through her battered body. She screamed in spite of herself. And dropped again to her knees.

Megan doubled over and tried to cry out, but there was no air. All the breath had been knocked free of her lungs. She seemed unable to move, but as Robin tried to pull herself up toward her, she swung the poker weakly, glancing a blow off her head. "Don't, you bitch," Megan wheezed. "I'll kill you."

Robin's vision clouded over again. She inhaled deeply, but her chest filled with swarms of stinging bees and wasps. She tried to cry out, to beg Megan to stop, to convince her that she was Robin. But she could only force a tiny whimper.

Gulping air, Megan landed another blow to her head. And another. Her eyes blazed diabolically as she swung the poker again and again.

Then over her shoulder toward the door, through the haze of her vision, Robin saw the shadow behind Megan's back. She fell heavily backward as another blow slammed into the useless arm, sending agony coursing through her body. She struggled to pull herself up into a half-sitting position, staring in disbelief at the two figures before her.

"*Oh dear Jesus!*" Stephanie screamed as she brought the straight backed chair down as hard as she could on Megan's head.

Megan collapsed forward on her face, striking her head on the corner of the coffee table as she went down. She stayed down. Stephanie stared mesmerized at the crumpled body.

For a time, there was only the sound of harsh, heavy breathing. At last, Robin forced herself to her knees, smothering the pain. She drew in as much air as her broken ribs would let her while she checked Megan's pulse.

"Don't say she's dead," Stephanie whispered. "Oh my God, Robin, don't say she's dead."

"She's just unconscious. Sit down. You look like you might faint."

Stephanie found the sofa. She lowered her head between her knees to fight off the waves of weakness. She looked up, her face deadly pale. With a groan, Robin pulled herself onto the sofa beside her.

"Find the phone," Robin said. "Call 911."

Fighting dizziness, Stephanie found it under an end table, and managed to say there was an emergency at Robin's address.

"Megan was going to kill me," Robin said. "You saved my life."

"She is a very sick woman," Stephanie said. "She needs the kind of intensive treatment she can only get in a hospital."

"Yes, I know. Les told me. It's like an awful dream."

"Les told me too — about her escape and all. He said you were out looking for her. I came over as soon as I could. I thought you might need some help if you found her and brought her home."

"I should have been more careful. I should have locked her in the bedroom," Robin said miserably. "I just didn't — couldn't — believe she could be like —

213

like she was tonight. Les told me she had threatened you with a knife but I . . ."

"Thought I was exaggerating?"

"Something like that." Robin shook her head and looked embarrassed.

"She would have killed me," Stephanie said, "If it hadn't been for those stupid fish of yours."

A look of confusion fell over Robin's face. "Fish?"

"Never mind," Stephanie said as they heard the siren of the ambulance drawing closer. "I'll explain it to you later."

* * * * *

"God, I wish I didn't have to go back to Washington tomorrow," Billie said. They were lying naked in Alice's king-size bed.

Alice sighed. "I wish finishing the Dexter Spencer business didn't mean not having you around every day."

"I'm glad it's over. We were lucky Roger Plank could lead us to the graves of Munsington and the woman. That more or less closed the case against him."

"That poor girl," Alice said. "That could have been Ruth."

"Or any of those other innocent people if we hadn't gotten them out in time. It's a good thing you got suspicious," Billie said. "Thank heaven everyone seems to be okay. Even your Alicia seems not to have suffered any permanent effects."

For a while they were quiet, lying on their backs, and holding hands.

At last Alice said, "And that awful Greg Rooney.

Thank God he's behind bars. What a despicable man!"

"There's a lot of evil in this world," Billie said.

"Do you ever think about quitting the agency?" Alice leaned over to kiss Billie on the neck.

"Not really. Can't you come to Washington with me this time?" She lightly kissed Alice's fingertips, then the tip of her nose, and her lips.

"I wish I could. I'll miss you as always. But there's still a lot for me to do here. The court docket is always full. And then there's the baby. Almost losing her like that has made me want to be close to her. At least for a while. I'll come up as soon as I can."

"I have something for you," Billie said. "To remember me by while we're apart." She opened the drawer of the night table and pulled out a box. "For once I even know where I put it."

Alice smiled. "You don't have to give me something to make me remember you. How could I forget?"

Billie opened the box. It was a large star-sapphire ring. "When I saw this, it reminded me of your eyes. I couldn't resist buying it for you."

"It's breathtaking," Alice said, slipping it on her finger. The ring lit up like exploding fireworks as she turned it to catch the light of the bedside lamp. She thanked Billie with a long kiss.

"I love you, my beautiful, beautiful blue eyes." Billie moved even closer. She cupped Alice's full breast and lifted it gently to her lips, then circled it with tiny kisses.

"That's all I really need to remember you by," Alice said. And she turned out the light.

* * * * *

Two months later a bellhop showed Stephanie and Robin to their suite in Bar Harbor, Maine. The air was cool and clean and smelled of pine needles. It was the first vacation for either of them in over a year.

The management had provided an iced bottle of champagne which they drank with a series of toasts made to Alice and Billie, to justice and peace, and to the full recovery of Evelyn Hightower.

Later they made love, being careful of Robin's healing arm, but also careful to do what pleased the other most. It felt like a rich, full homecoming, and they were sated afterwards.

They lay silent for a while, arms and legs entwined. At last Stephanie said, "Do you really think we can forget the past? We've hurt each other so much."

"Maybe we've grown up a little. Even our lovemaking is . . . I don't know, better. Different."

"Do you suppose it's youth that makes us want everyone else to be just like we are? To think exactly the way we think? That's what I wanted from you."

"Maybe it's fear," Robin said. "Fear that what we are is somehow wrong. Seems like the more people we can find who are just like us, the more sure we can be that what we are is okay. Must be human nature."

"I think we can both want different things from life and still have each other too."

"Can I tell you something?" Robin asked.

"Something I've always wanted? I've never told anybody."

"Try me," Stephanie said.

"You might think I'm weird, but I've always wanted to make love in a room with mirrors on the ceiling."

"Mirrors!"

Robin grinned. "That's different, huh?"

Stephanie leaned over and kissed her lightly on the mouth. "That's one kind of difference I hadn't counted on! But if that's what you want, and you can find a place like that, I guess I'll go with you."

"I want you," Robin said. "Mirrors or no mirrors."

"And I want you."

"Then that's all that matters."

Stephanie folded Robin in her arms. And the whole world became no larger than the expanse of their two bodies.

A few of the publications of
THE NAIAD PRESS, INC.
P.O. Box 10543 • Tallahassee, Florida 32302
Phone (904) 539-5965
Mail orders welcome. Please include 15% postage.

COP OUT by Claire McNab. 208 pp. 4th Det. Insp. Carol Ashton mystery.
ISBN 0-941483-84-3 $8.95

LODESTAR by Phyllis Horn. 224 pp. Romantic, fast-moving adventure.
ISBN 0-941483-83-5   8.95

THE BEVERLY MALIBU by Katherine V. Forrest. 288 pp. A Kate Delafield Mystery. 3rd in a series. (HC)   ISBN 0-941483-47-9   16.95
Paperback   ISBN 0-941483-48-7   9.95

THAT OLD STUDEBAKER by Lee Lynch. 272 pp. Andy's affair with Regina and her attachment to her beloved car.
ISBN 0-941483-82-7   9.95

PASSION'S LEGACY by Lori Paige. 224 pp. Sarah is swept into the arms of Augusta Pym in this delightful historical romance.
ISBN 0-941483-81-9   8.95

THE PROVIDENCE FILE by Amanda Kyle Williams. 256 pp. Second espionage thriller featuring lesbian agent Madison McGuire
ISBN 0-941483-92-4   8.95

I LEFT MY HEART by Jaye Maiman. 320 pp. A Robin Miller Mystery. First in a series.
ISBN 0-941483-72-X   9.95

THE PRICE OF SALT by Patricia Highsmith (writing as Claire Morgan). 288 pp. Classic lesbian novel, first issued in 1952 . . . acknowledged by its author under her own, very famous, name.
ISBN 1-56280-003-5   8.95

SIDE BY SIDE by Isabel Miller. 256 pp. From beloved author of *Patience and Sarah*.
ISBN 0-941483-77-0   8.95

SOUTHBOUND by Sheila Ortiz Taylor. 240 pp. Hilarious sequel to *Faultline*.
ISBN 0-941483-78-9   8.95

STAYING POWER: LONG TERM LESBIAN COUPLES by Susan E. Johnson. 352 pp. Joys of coupledom.
ISBN 0-941-483-75-4   12.95

These are just a few of the many Naiad Press titles — we are the oldest and largest lesbian/feminist publishing company in the world. Please request a complete catalog. We offer personal service; we encourage and welcome direct mail orders from individuals who have limited access to bookstores carrying our publications.